PRAISE FOR LOST SEEDS

"An intriguing and interesting read. *Lost Seeds: The Beginning* is imaginatively conceived, vividly written, and gives a new insight into the complexity of being Black in America. Perfect for a book club discussion!"
—Rita P. Mitchell, author, speaker, and empowerment coach

LOST SEEDS

LOST SEEDS

THE BEGINNING

Teresa Mosley Sebastian

Dominion Asset Publishing

This is a work of fiction. Names, characters, organizations, places, events, and incidents are either products of the author's imagination or are used fictitiously.

Copyright © 2023 by Teresa Mosley Sebastian

All rights reserved.

No part of this book may be reproduced, or stored in a retrieval system, or transmitted in any form or by any means, electronic, mechanical, photocopying, recording, or otherwise, without express written permission of the publisher.

Published by Dominion Asset Publishing, Nashville
www.teresamosleysebastian.com

GIRL FRIDAY
PRODUCTIONS

Edited and designed by Girl Friday Productions
www.girlfridayproductions.com

Cover design: Avital David
Cover illustration: Alon David
Project management: Reshma Kooner
Editorial production: Jaye Whitney Debber

ISBN (paperback): 979-8-9884670-0-7
ISBN (ebook): 979-8-9884670-1-4

Library of Congress Control Number: 2023913247

This book is dedicated to my husband, Steve; daughter, Simone; son, George; and granddaughter, Amaya.

CONTENTS

Chapter 1	New Beginnings (1928)	1
Chapter 2	The Briscos (1865–1914)	4
Chapter 3	Betsey (1914)	11
Chapter 4	Dub and Mae (1915)	14
Chapter 5	Timothy (1915)	19
Chapter 6	Changes (1918–1922)	26
Chapter 7	Timothy and Kate (1923–1924)	33
Chapter 8	Betsey's Wrath (1924)	46
Chapter 9	Cultivating Life (1924)	60
Chapter 10	The Dare (1924)	68
Chapter 11	Comings and Goings (1924)	77
Chapter 12	Moving On (1924)	89
Chapter 13	Cost of Desires (1924–1925)	105
Chapter 14	Promises (1925–1926)	114
Chapter 15	Ambition (1926)	126
Chapter 16	The Ticket (1926)	137
Chapter 17	The Identity (1926)	140
Chapter 18	The Destination (1926–1927)	144
Chapter 19	Success (1927)	156
Chapter 20	The Room (1927–1928)	159
Chapter 21	Abingdon (1928–1929)	171
Chapter 22	Underground (1929)	176

Acknowledgments 182
About the Author 187

CHAPTER 1

NEW BEGINNINGS (1928)

As Dub did a regular midnight walk around the perimeter of his yard, a dark figure appeared at the end of the driveway. It approached with a familiar gait. Dub tensed every muscle in his body and stuffed his hands in his pants pockets. Fists clenched.

"Hey, brother," he said.

"Hey, Dub." Tim's grip tightened on the laundry bag containing his only possessions.

"Mama sent that letter over two years ago. Said you were doing some bad stuff."

Tim responded with a nervous chuckle and shrugged. A moment of silence extended as if an entire year were going by. A brief wind blew into his face, filling the void.

"Some stories are never fully told. The rest manifest through our illness and perversities," Tim said.

With a raised voice, Dub said, "Stop the bullshit talk, college boy."

"That's why even you escaped Morriston and didn't look

back, Dub. You couldn't face the past anymore. For me, I couldn't live in the past, and that's why I didn't get off the train here in Abingdon, Illinois, back then."

Tim gave the bare minimum facts about the last two years, and Dub gave an even briefer update on their family.

Tim's shoulders curled inward. After taking a deep breath and dropping his head, he said, "What else can I tell you right now?"

The brothers stood in the darkness lit by the moon. Each scanning the night shadows without acknowledging the presence of anything around them, including each other.

Dub finally faced Tim dispassionately, breathed in deeply, and explained the meager accommodations at the back of his property.

Tim ambled to his new residence. A single step and modest stoop led to the shack's thick mahogany door that Dub had retrieved from the curb of a mansion-sized plantation house on the other side of town. The crawl space beneath the windowless, dark wooden structure suspended on twelve-inch stilts helped keep the building cool inside.

The next morning, the starkness of life came into view from slivers of sunlight oozing through the slat walls. Tim lit one of the two oil lamps hanging from the ceiling.

A scan of the room revealed little. A beige wardrobe steamer trunk leaned in the far corner. A small table accompanied a single chair. The cot and its matted feather pillow challenged his back, prompting him to stretch to release the tightened muscles. A smoke-stained blue kerosene heater with bear claws for feet stood in the opposite corner.

He avoided spending time observing himself in the mirror, the only item on the wall. Walking to a pedestal topped by a white porcelain bowl, he lowered his head and closed his eyes as if in prayer. Upon opening them, tears obstructed his view of the surroundings. With surrender, he reached toward the floor for the tin bucket beneath the stand and made the first trip to the well, beginning the cycle of days to come.

CHAPTER 2

THE BRISCOS (1865–1914)

Tim and Dub's parents—Tuttle, born the year slavery was abolished, and Betsey, who Tuttle married in 1885 when she was only twelve—had fourteen children in all. The couple raised them in a one-room wood-frame home Tuttle built with his own hands.

Although a free slave on paper, Tuttle still carried Green Creek plantation owner Hatch Brisco's last name. Living and working in southern Alabama on the slave compound where Tuttle could find work came at the price of debt servitude—which was not much different from slavery—not to mention the abuse of the women in Tuttle's family and excessive consumption of alcohol to drown the pain.

Any explanation of Dub's and Tim's lives as brothers must start at the source of their existence. Dublin, called Dub for short, entered the world in 1900. Timothy came along seven years later. Although Dub was on the darker side like his daddy, Tim was olive complexioned and even more Mediterranean looking than his mother. The circumstances of their mother's pregnancy created features that led some to mistake Tim as white.

***

"Dub, go out behind the cottage and find some wood for the fire so your mama and sisters can cook something," Tuttle said to the fourteen-year-old.

"Why do I have to?" Dub said from the hay-filled cot he shared with his brothers. "I'm tired and my hands are raw from work today."

"Boy, did you hear what I said?" Tuttle stood swaying with the bottle of spirits in his hand.

A park-bench-length burlap sack filled with hay sat in a dimly lit corner. The youngest children perched on top, huddled together so body heat and brief sprays of warm air from the fireplace turned the corner into a warm haven.

"I'll get it," said Zeke, the oldest son at home at eighteen years of age, exiting the corner from a low stool where he had been reading a book to Tim, the last-born child.

Tuttle walked forward, staring into Dub's eyes. "Sit your butt down, Zeke, I wasn't talking to you. Your brother must think he's grown and can talk however he wants to me. You grown, Dub?"

"No, sir."

Tuttle grabbed an ax handle leaning on the hearth.

"I work my ass off all day too and put up with Master Hatch's bullshit just to put food in your mouth," Tuttle said, shaking the handle. "Can you do that? Let's see just how grown you are." He swung the weapon at Dub's head as he had many times before. Dub ducked and Tuttle fell forward onto the floor.

A fist banged multiple times on the door. The entire family froze.

Muffled sounds of laughter came from outside.

"Sounds like Hatch with some men," Betsey said in a whisper. "Tuttle, get up off the floor. Do something."

Betsey pulled all the girls behind her, and the older boys stood in front of Betsey. From the safe corner, Tim's whimpers filled the room.

"Shush your mouth, boy," Betsey whispered forcefully to the child.

Tim curled up in a ball, covering his ears, his eyes riveted toward the front of the house.

The door shook, but the lock kept it sealed. Tuttle struggled to stand. His feet fought each other as neither ankle seemed to support his weight.

"Who is it?" he said, slurring his words.

"You know who it is. Open this door," Hatch said.

"We're preparing for bed, Master Hatch."

"Open this door, Tuttle, if you know what's good for you."

"Please, sir, my daughters are indisposed," Betsey said.

Tuttle crawled to the dining table, levering himself up to stand. Mouth agape, he quickly scanned the room as if to count the number of family members in the hope that he would have the same amount in the end. Straightening his shoulders back, he appeared to sober.

A strange voice outside the door said, "Isn't that convenient."

Hatch banged on the door again. "That's it, Tuttle. You got it coming for defying me, you lowlife drunk."

The butt of a rifle broke through one of the few windows in the house, spraying glass inside. A broad hand followed to release the lock, and the thick leather sole of a boot kicked open the door. Tuttle rushed to grab the ax handle he'd used on Dub and swung it in Hatch's direction.

Hatch turned the rifle around to aim the barrel directly at Betsey. The butt of the rifle lay over his shoulder, on top of a white cotton nightgown with lace he'd brought for Betsey to wear for his pleasure. Everyone in the room paused, and quiet took over.

"There's the mammie of my bastards. How many do we have now, Betsey?" Hatch said. "Let's see if I can breed you again for one more body to work my fields. I got a couple of poker buddies with me for these girls too. Now, Tuttle, you just take those boys and little ones out of here like you're supposed to and leave me with these women."

Tuttle's forehead furrowed, with deep creases forming. Each crease contained a river of sweat emptying as he heaved violently to contain the rage. Every inch of his body visibly tightened, fixated on Hatch. He lifted his fist slowly and slapped it against his own leg.

"Tuttle," Betsey whispered, wrapping her arms around herself.

"Grab the babies and let's go," Tuttle said to Zeke.

These were the atrocities Tuttle's kids experienced and internalized very early on.

The youngsters and boys followed Tuttle up the dirt road. No one spoke. The only noise became the occasional sniffling from Tim and the crunching of rock beneath the family's feet.

The pack slowed, approaching the destination they visited on these occasions. The church steps. Tuttle sat and pulled Tim to his lap and cradled the boy as he would an infant. Tim's body shuddered, releasing the noises he'd wanted to make before. The other children sat on the ground. Some played in the dirt, some pulled up blades of grass. Dub traced the constellations in the sky with his fingers. But no one spoke a word.

An hour later, Tuttle, the boys, and the youngsters returned to the cabin. The daughters huddled together in their nightshirts, knees to their chests and faces tear stained. Betsey stood dry eyed and stoic at the fireplace, heating a pot of water and cutting pieces of lye soap. She quietly handed a rag to each girl as if carrying out a sacred ceremony after combing her own hair and putting on a clean dress. Igniting in the fire was the white nightgown. Tuttle saw the empty bottle of liquor on the table.

Betsey said, "Yes, I drank it all. It's all I could do."

"My debts are paid here," Tuttle said. "I'll handle whatever comes next, but not from this man. Betsey, get our stuff together. We're heading to Morriston, Alabama, like our other family members, to live the way freed slaves are supposed to."

The next evening, Tuttle decided to act on the plan he'd contemplated for years. Guided by a cousin's letter and map with safe havens, Tuttle rounded up the nine children still living at home, Betsey, and their possessions in the darkness of night to avoid danger or questions about the purpose of their excursion.

Stealthily and with determination, the crew started the trek north. Betsey and the youngest children rode in a pushcart, and the older children and Tuttle flanked the sides of a wagon hooked to two mules.

At daybreak, the family secreted themselves among the cover of an abandoned barn. On the second night of travel, they cautiously ventured further northward.

More than halfway to their destination, two broad-shouldered men riding horses branded with the Hatch plantation insignia on the hindquarters emerged, riding southward out of the darkness on a narrow dirt road lined with tall trees. Each man carried a rifle propped across his lap. Other than a brief nod and tip of the hat, the men did not react to the family, nor did a word pass between the two horsemen.

Huddled together, the family proceeded tentatively as the horsemen continued their journey. Tuttle slowed to patrol the wagon and his family from the rear while Zeke guided the mules.

Farther down the road, with a signal from one horseman to the other, the men stopped their horses. They swiftly dismounted and scurried into the bushes, stalking the family from afar for a quarter mile.

Small kerosene lanterns held by Tuttle's other boys failed to illuminate the impending danger. Suddenly, a stampede of footsteps emerged from the shrubbery and approached the family, and the silhouettes of the horsemen were revealed: one carrying a bludgeon and the other a rifle.

"This is from Hatch Brisco," one of the men said. "You thought you'd leave without paying him the money you owe?"

Betsey corralled the children. She whispered to them, "Douse the lanterns. Hold hands and follow me." The boys quickly turned the knobs, shutting off the flames in the lamps. She ran a distance into the night toward thick brush and lay down, motioning for the children to lay around her.

As Tuttle turned around, poised to fight, his world went dark. The killers stood around laughing and continuing to batter his head with the stock of their shotgun.

Betsey held Zeke's and Dub's coats tightly while the boys clawed at the dirt, attempting to lunge into the fight to save their father. The horsemen finally tired and rode away, celebrating their feat. After some hours spent afraid to reveal their whereabouts, dawn broke and the family found themselves alone, with Tuttle hanging from a tall, majestic poplar tree.

Zeke, with fortitude, retrieved a knife and shovel, climbed the tree, and cut down the lifeless body. After directing Zeke's younger brothers, including Dub and Tim, to dig a hole, Betsey pulled out a Bible and prayed, attempting to perform a dignified burial. The girls made a cross out of broken branches strewn about on the ground and picked flowers, then threw petals in the grave and placed the cross in the ground as a makeshift headstone.

The Briscos, minus their patriarch, continued the flight to Morriston, Alabama, a town of around thirty-five hundred people. In contrast to the overt oppressions of Green Creek, Morriston bustled with activity during the week, from early morning to midafternoon when the railroad trains came through, delivering various goods and commodities to the factories and picking up cottonseed, spools of yarn, and fabric.

Due to the busy weekdays, residents rested on the weekend. Families went to church, took casual strolls, and waved at other acquaintances relaxing on front porches. Yet and still, beneath the pleasantries, a railroad track and the downtown split Morriston into two worlds—Black and white, with unseen boundaries to friendships.

After the Briscos arrived, the children had no time to grieve Tuttle, or experience the joys of being young. Any Brisco female over ten years old found work cleaning houses, and the males held odd jobs. To save money, the family stayed with relatives before moving into their own home in Low Orchard, where the Black residents of Morriston lived.

Betsey controlled the Briscos' world. Each Sabbath included Sunday school, a sermon, and gathering outside with congregants, capped off with a full dinner table of food from the garden. These peaceful Sundays failed to mask six days of toil consisting of school, manual labor, and Betsey's occasional evening drinking binges followed by beatings for breaking her rules. The new existence managed to change the venue yet did not eliminate Betsey's memories of Green Creek and Tuttle's brutal death.

CHAPTER 3

BETSEY (1914)

The house Betsey purchased in Low Orchard became a respite compared to Green Creek. Like most other homes in that community, it contained the bare minimum necessities to live—stark white-painted walls, two bedrooms, wash closet, living room, and kitchen, all sandwiched between a back and front stoop to sit and watch the comings and goings in the neighborhood.

Settling in Morriston gave Betsey a new start. But two things did not change. During the day, she and the children worked tirelessly to put money in a glass mason jar for savings. And at night, as for Tuttle, liquor released Betsey's anger. She targeted the child who either happened to be in her sight at the moment of intoxication or failed to drop coins into the jar within proximity for Betsey to hear the clang of the money hitting the glass. Much like in Green Creek, the youngest sought the corners of the home for solace.

A picture of Tuttle hung in the hallway, stern faced, standing in the middle of the family. One arm spread around Zeke's shoulder and the other around Dub's, as if protecting his brood. Sometimes the face appeared serene. Betsey stood at the portrait each morning, deciding Tuttle's disposition and her own. Often settling on emptiness.

Without Tuttle, loneliness pushed Betsey beyond the front and back porches out to the neighborhood bars. Going to the nightclub gave her a reprieve from the household and lack of money and gave her hope of finding a replacement for Tuttle.

On those evenings, in the bedroom she shared with the girls, her long, wavy hair was released from the hairpins, draped halfway down her back, then re-pinned into twirled spirals over her shoulder. Thick red lipstick contrasted her bright olive skin color while accenting the fullness of her lips.

From the bottom of a steamer trunk emerged a tea gown with an ornate lace, beaded torso and deep plunging neckline. A gift from Master Hatch. The image and purpose of her costume reminded Betsey of the first time she'd donned the dress, eight years ago.

***

After drinking with friends and sons, Hatch sent the overseer to summon Betsey to a cabin at the back of the plantation. Hatch kept the cabin for himself and his sons for such encounters, with a room that was a replica of his bedchamber in the main house.

When demanding that Betsey put on the dress, he said, "My wife grew too fat for this. She said it made her look like a whore. Let's see if it makes you look like a whore."

The bodice cinched Betsey's chest like a tight corset. Hatch immediately grabbed her blossoming breasts and plunged his face into the cleavage, knocking her over onto the four-post mahogany bed. The bottom half of the dress rose to her expanding waist, where it remained until Hatch finished with her. He did not care that she'd become pregnant with Tim months before and her breasts held milk in preparation to feed their child.

***

When Betsey and Tuttle fled Green Creek, she understood the value of the dress and packed it without Tuttle's knowledge, hoping one day to sell it and help start a new life for the family. The dress now helped to make money in the same way Hatch had extracted his pleasure for free.

The moment she stepped into the bar, the sway of her hips accentuated the shimmer from the beads. She canvassed the room and held the gaze of the men who nodded in return as an indication of willingness to part with meaningful amounts of coins for her time.

Over the years, despite maintaining the same weight, age and excessive alcohol took their toll. Increasing frustration set in too, when the willingness of paramours to pay for her time did not result in marriage. She fought single men who rejected her because of the number of children living at her home. She beat on married men who refused to leave their wives. She assaulted wives who caught her with their husbands.

In Low Orchard, salacious news circulated fast. Even the children witnessed Betsey's deteriorating reputation. To compensate, she relied on the children for financial support, spent more time controlling Tim, focused on maintaining a spotless home, and attended church.

Eventually, within a year, most of the Brisco children escaped Betsey's anger and severed ties, choosing to live with other family in other towns or, in the case of Zeke and Dub, to launch their own lives in Morriston, leaving Tim to manage alone.

CHAPTER 4

DUB AND MAE (1915)

Dub's departure from Betsey's home began when Mae, a uniquely beautiful petite girl with long hair worn in a bun, captured his attention. Mae came from a prominent Creole family. After her father's death, she moved from New Orleans, Louisiana, to Morriston, Alabama, with her aunt and uncle.

Dub's suave approach, with colorful bouquets picked from the side of the road and buttoned-up shirts, impressed Mae. He could elevate her to the higher lifestyle she'd glimpsed in New Orleans before her father died. Two months after they met, the fifteen-year-olds married and moved in with Mae's relatives.

The couple needed money, so Mae found work in the laundry room of the biggest hotel in town. Dub landed a job in the textile factory as a janitor.

The lack of food and accommodations for the newlyweds soon made living with family impossible. After Easter Sunday services, they saw an advertisement board at the church listing a room for rent. The couple immediately ran to the home and paid the first week's fee.

The two-story, four-bedroom house filled with fine furniture belonged to Miss Clara. She still lived in her childhood home at sixty years old; she'd never wed or had children. She was a child when slavery ended. Her father, a renowned leatherworker, and her mother, a prominent pastry chef, prospered and built the grandest house in Low Orchard. Clara lived a life of comfort. Her loneliness came because her parents believed no young man had prospects equal to her high school education or offered her the financial stability her parents provided.

***

Dub and Mae, and less than one year later, their first-born child, Dublin Junior, who they called Junie, became Clara's adopted family. Each Sunday, the young family and Miss Clara sat on the porch, watching neighbors stroll by. Some waved, some nodded, and others stopped to engage in gossip with Clara and Mae.

"I love this house, Dub. It's so grand. One day we'll have a place just like this. Don't you agree?"

"Sure," Dub said, turning his head.

"But you're seventeen with a baby," Miss Clara said.

"We can do it, Dub," Mae fervently replied.

Dub sighed and said, "First I need to work as many jobs as I can."

Mae returned to work, accelerating their savings, by taking Junie with her. Each weekday at five o'clock in the morning, the sun barely peering over the horizon, she served her son and husband breakfast. Afterward, hoisting the child into a back sling, she walked the one mile to town.

Passing the hotel entrance, she turned into a narrow dark alley, avoiding homeless people whose legs sprawled into the walkway, their torsos hidden between garbage bins. Each one briefly popped forward asking for food. Mae kept one arm twisted behind her back holding the infant. She stuck the other hand out in a stop-sign fashion, a cloth bag filled with diapers and food fixed firmly on her shoulder. She continued at a brisk pace, occasionally glancing behind at the begging eyes following her footsteps.

Finally reaching the back door labeled "Laborers," she sighed. "Little guy, we made it safely again. No muggers."

A single beam of light illuminated the vestibule and short passageway with stairs descending to a cement-block cellar below the hotel.

"Good morning, ladies," Mae said upon arriving at the destination.

All the women wore white cotton dress uniforms. Hair tied back in the required buns and a black headband.

The laundry room painted in all white reflected the image of cleanliness. The room encompassed one big space, hot and humid with no sunshine. The only fresh air came from small windows near the ceiling. Pipes, beams, and lights hung from above, brightening the area in an industrial setting, and steep posts rose from the floor to support the fifty-guest-room structure.

On one side of the laundry stood four long tables for sorting dirty linens. Canvas bins with wheels dotted the space, ready to be used to transfer bundles.

At the far end of the room stood manually operated washing machines with rollers to squeeze water from the cotton fibers. A team of ladies waited attentively around the machines to unload cleaned items and cart them to the next set of hands.

Fingers eagerly waited at the next station, with three or more wooden clips within their grasp. Clothespins quickly released and the springs snapped shut, hanging the finished linen to dry on ropes draped from one side of the room to the other.

The opposite end of the cellar housed two rows of four

ironing boards and irons. Pots of water hung above the workers to dampen the fabric, the key to crisply starched and pressed bedding, curtains, tablecloths, and napkins.

"Morning, Mae," said the chorus settling in for a day's work. The ladies smiled and cooed at the baby.

"Here's our guy," Fanny, the lead launderer, sang, squeezing Junie's toes. "But Mae, you can't carry him around on your back all day. I had my husband bind together some extra wood from our yard fence into a child's playpen. I put a soft wool blanket inside on the floor. It's in the safest place in this room. See over there behind the folding table away from the machines and irons? That's not too far from your workstation but not too close either, because of the irons."

"Thanks."

"You're welcome, because you're the best steam presser we have. You wash the sheets and uniforms whiter than white and then get them stiff like a flat fresh piece of paper."

Mae continued bringing Junie to the hotel laundry. At nine months, the baby grew more active. One day, while the ladies fervently bustled around, the child shook the enclosure hard enough that the ropes holding one side snapped. A space expanded large enough for Junie to quietly crawl toward Mae.

The sound of heavy metal hitting a concrete floor reverberated throughout the room, bringing everyone and all activity to a startled standstill. Junie wailed.

"My baby," Mae screamed, looking at his crib.

A strip of fencing leaned askew, exposing the gap in the playpen.

"I got him," declared Fanny, scooping him up only inches away from a hot iron that had fallen from Fanny's station. "I can't believe it! He got out of that cage. Something hit my board here and the iron suddenly crashed to the floor."

While Fanny checked the baby for injuries, Mae ran over to rub his head.

"I'm sorry, Fanny. I guess keeping him around the equipment is too dangerous now."

"Yes. We need new arrangements."

"I can't risk bringing my baby here anymore."

"I'll talk to the manager and ask him to send bags of clean tablecloths and napkins to your house for pressing. You're too good for us to lose. We'll pay a price for each bag you iron," Fanny said, passing Junie to Mae. "First I'll call the janitor down here to fix the playpen so we can finish up today."

"That's a much better idea," Mae said, hugging the child. "Dub and I couldn't handle it if anything bad happened to this baby."

CHAPTER 5

TIMOTHY (1915)

As the only remaining child living with Betsey, eight-year-old Tim spent time working and taking long walks at night alone. Some evenings, he sneaked across town to Upper Orchard, the side of Morriston where wealthy white families lived. He peered through the windows, hoping to learn how to improve himself.

Over time, Tim witnessed a lifestyle unlike anything he'd experienced on the Green Creek plantation or in Low Orchard. The secret trips to Upper Orchard were like attending a theater. One house on Jackson Street drew him back several nights each week to catch the next scene in the family's life. The main character, a young girl his age, with olive skin and long black curly hair, looked much like Tim.

He lingered in the darkness next to a large walnut tree much broader than his tall, thin frame. It gave him a good view into the parlor where the family gathered after dinner.

A plush brown couch sat facing the marble fireplace. Directly on either side sat matching chairs, one for the mother and one for the father to relax in while conversing with the girl. A part of the dining room contained a long formal waxed wood table with ornate candlesticks, lit by the brown-skinned butler each night before the family strolled into the room after cocktails in the parlor. A broad, winding staircase lined with a fine Persian rug, and handrails made of decorative iron, created opulent scenery through a distant archway. Paintings of grand ancestors dressed in expensive silks and satins imported from other countries hung on the walls.

The scenes in Upper Orchard contrasted with Tim's sparsely furnished home, where Betsey sat on the back porch waiting for him to return from school or work and leave again. A bottle of whiskey rested on the ground, wedged between the wooden step and a concrete block holding up the stoop.

Hearing Zeke's footsteps moving from the front door into the kitchen, Betsey leaned toward the back door, saying, "Food is in the icebox and bread is on the table under the baking cloth. Don't forget to put money in the jar from your week's pay."

Of the thirteen children living outside of Betsey's home, Zeke and Dub were the only ones remaining in Morriston. Yet only Zeke routinely visited Tim and Betsey.

"Why do you think I stopped by, Mama?" Zeke said, arriving from his job at a cotton baling factory. He grabbed a slice of bread, spread butter on top, and jammed it in his mouth. "When was the last time Dub showed his face in here?"

"I never see him since he married that uppity Creole bitch. She made him divorce his responsibility to this house. He doesn't give me shit although he makes good money. That wife of his is too expensive for his wallet," Betsey said, leaning toward the back door.

"And that's another reason I don't have a wife right now." Zeke waved goodbye to Tim, who was just coming home from his after-school job and heading out to his second place of work.

"Any money, Tim?" Betsey said, picking up the whiskey bottle to take a swig.

"Yes, ma'am," Tim said softly.

"What'd you say?" Betsey asked.

"Yes, ma'am." Tim dutifully dropped coins into the money jar and placed his hat on the hook by the back door. Assuring Betsey was not within view, he slyly removed from his pocket a measuring stick purchased from the hardware store on his way home. Lifting it to the ceiling, he gleefully scanned the numbers as he slid his hand along the straight edges.

"This is what I need," he said.

Tim positioned the ruler on the kitchen table, then proceeded to the icebox to remove a freshly baked chicken sliced into thin pieces. He delicately placed each slice on an old clay serving dish, arranging them from smallest to largest, then encircled the chicken with wedges of tomato and sprinkled salt on top. Last, he raised the white cloth off the bread like a magician preparing to perform.

With a stiff back, he turned to gather a place setting of cutlery, a cotton napkin, and a dinner plate from the cupboard. His right hand waved the ruler like a wand, and his left hand moved the plate in front of the chair to be served. Then, after lining up the ruler above the plate, both hands worked to lay the fork to the left and the knife and spoon to the right. Fingers folded the napkin into a diamond shape, then placed it to the left of the fork.

He positioned the ruler along the rim of the table to ensure appropriate space between the edge and the bottom of the place setting. He glided lightly to the cabinet, and his fingers gently removed a glass from the shelf, filled it with water from a pitcher, and lightly settled the drink to the top right of the plate. The same fingers lifted the stick and waved it over the table with satisfaction.

"That's it. That's what it feels like," he said as he sat in the chair, hands continuing to nervously tweak and perfect the masterpiece.

Betsey stood wavering in the doorway, watching the precision of Tim's efforts.

"What the hell are you doing?" she said.

"Nothing, Mama."

"You trying to be some houseboy on the plantation?" she said. "Where'd Zeke go? Did he leave any money?"

"I'm . . . not sure, ma'am. After chugging down the butter sandwich, he left."

Betsey stumbled over to the shelf where the mason jar had sat since the day they moved into the home. Nodding with satisfaction, she winked at Tim, walked over, and rubbed his curls.

"My body needs to lay down. I sure wish your daddy was here to handle you boys."

Betsey steadied herself for the walk to the living room and plopped down on the sofa. Tim waited until her eyes closed before he sat straight up in the chair, laid the napkin on his leg, and proceeded to eat with one hand in his lap, like the families in Upper Orchard.

The next morning, Tim arose earlier than normal and slipped on his clothes quietly.

"Where are you going?" Zeke asked from the kitchen.

"Why? You aren't my keeper."

"Why? Because no one is usually up this early when I stop by for breakfast. That's why."

"Then none of your business. Why don't you eat at your own place with whatever woman you're screwing, then you won't have to worry about what I'm doing?"

Leaving out the back door, Tim ran the five blocks downtown to the library adjacent to the town square. Through the thick-wood-and-stained-glass door, he saw the lights turn on one section at a time. He jumped, hearing a stack of newspapers land inches from his feet.

"You're peering through that window like they've got hot oatmeal to feed you." The boy stopped his bicycle with one foot on the pedal and the other on the ground, still balancing the newspapers in a satchel hanging over the back wheel.

"Shut up. Your papers are what I'm waiting for."

"You better not touch them, Tim. That librarian inside will have you arrested if you take one before she puts them in the library."

"I know! You don't need to tell me. I just want to read the want ads."

"Well, my route is taken, and I'm leaving now so I don't lose it. Everything in this bag needs delivering before school starts. See you in class."

The library door opened.

"Oh my, you scared me, boy. What do you want?" the librarian said, blocking the doorway.

Tim looked past the woman into a long hallway lined with intricately carved dark wooden pillars on each side separating rows of bookshelves. The three sets of card catalog cabinets guarded the entry way to the stacks awaiting visitors to browse the contents. Marble floors shone from the previous night's janitorial service. He inhaled. The smell of wax seeped through the opened door.

"Just the morning newspaper. Sorry, ma'am," he said, taking a step back.

"OK. Let me take them inside and lay them out."

"Yes, ma'am."

Tim followed her inside, walking at least six feet behind. Occasionally, she paused to straighten a book on a shelf, adjust a chair beneath a table, or move the tabletop bust of a historical figure. He paused when she paused, never breaking the proper distance. Herringbone flooring carved a pathway to a section of newspaper racks, and a high-top desk awaited the arrival of a librarian.

After laying everything on the counter, the librarian handed Tim a newspaper and pointed to the far corner upstairs at a sign labeled "Coloreds." She never uttered a word.

Tim nodded and said, "Thank you, ma'am." The librarian turned and walked swiftly back to the front desk of the library to attend to other patrons awaiting her guidance. As he climbed the stairs, the sounds of the librarian's shoes clacking on the floor echoed throughout the quiet. Tim stopped and turned around to determine if she was following him. Seeing the librarian still walking in the opposite direction, he took the paper to the second floor. His fingers ran down the advertisements, lips mouthing the words. All movement seemed to stop when he arrived at the desired destination.

Butler Assistant Wanted in Upper Orchard for Benson Family—Evening Hours Only.

After school, Tim ran home to wash his face and put on clean clothes, then walked to the address in the advertisement. Along the way he dabbed his face and armpits dry from the heat and humidity. Reaching the address, he stood at the wrought-iron gate that led down a short brick driveway. A gardener stood up, waved, and pointed toward an open door to the back of the house, where several wait staff lounged, taking a break.

"You're here for the butler assistant job?"

"Yes. Who do I talk to?" Tim asked.

"Me, Larford Taylor, but call me Mr. Larry," said a regal-looking man dressed in white gloves and a black suit. "Can you do formal servicing? How old are you?"

"Eight, and I can show you if you let me come into the kitchen."

Tim performed the same demonstration he had practiced the night before in his own home.

"You're mighty tall for eight, but you're hired. Be here tomorrow at five sharp. But look, boy, don't be fooled. A butler's duties appear less tedious and backbreaking than field jobs or delivering groceries and cleaning toilets. But here, you must be invisible, otherwise you're gone. Understood?"

"Yes, sir."

At home, Tim continued to practice the etiquette of the wealthy homes. By accepting an invisible existence, he experienced a family together, sharing laughs, smiles, and touching, unlike his reality at home. Upper Orchard was Tim's sole escape from Betsey's world.

CHAPTER 6

CHANGES (1918–1922)

After two years at Miss Clara's, and a second son named Matthew, Dub and Mae had saved enough money to buy a house.

With few possessions, the move to the bungalow with two bedrooms, a living room, and a kitchen proceeded swiftly. The adults occupied one bedroom, and the two boys slept in the other. A small closet fit a tub and a pedestal with a bowl for bathing, and an outhouse stood in the backyard for the toilet. Curtains for the house and assistance with decorating using grand old furniture came from Clara. As a special gift to his wife, Dub built a mailbox designed to be a miniature replica of the actual house.

At the age of eighteen, Dub had all the responsibility of a man and the desire to make Green Creek a figment of the past. He held multiple jobs, while Mae continued ironing laundry for the hotel from their home and birthed their first girl, Bernadette, who they called Bernie.

***

Seven years of marriage made each day comfortably predictable to Dub, in contrast to his earlier life with Betsey and Green Creek. After enjoying a hot breakfast prepared by his wife, he left the house at five o'clock each morning, snack bag in hand, to work at the textile factory. He returned home for lunch at one o'clock in the afternoon, then continued to his second job, cleaning O'Malley's General Store, at two o'clock and worked until nine at night.

On Saturdays, he made repairs to their small house, helped supervise the offspring, spent time in the vegetable garden, and fished to put extra food on the table. Sundays encompassed worship and picnics with neighbors and church members.

***

Mae enjoyed the Sunday community picnics, taking great care to be the most stylish woman at the outing. In anticipation of the upcoming Sunday picnic celebrating the first day of summer, she made a new cotton dress from sheets discarded by the hotel and bought orange ribbon to make a colorful belt with a large bow in the back.

The day of the excursion to Crystal Lake on the western edge of Morriston, Mae fixed a picnic basket. She also packed crisp linen for the food, and a blanket for the children to lie down. Dub helped six-year-old Junie get dressed and pick out a toy to share with other children. The last piece of preparation included getting the youngest children ready: two-year-old Amaya, four-year-old Bernie, and five-year-old Matthew.

With all the necessities in hand, the Briscos proudly paraded to the outskirts of town. Mae carried Amaya in a back sling, Junie held Matthew's and Bernie's hands, and Dub hauled the food and a bag with the linens and blanket. Families regularly gathered at the lake, but like everything else, two distinct picnic areas existed, and people knew where they belonged along the sandy edge of the translucent blue water.

"OK, everyone, let's catch our breath. My goodness, it's hot today. Just traveling here tired me out," Mae said. "Hon, can you pull that blanket out of the bag? I want to lay the babies down for a nap."

She busied herself prepping the picnic spot near others from the neighborhood and attended to Bernie who had a slight cold. Matthew and Amaya fell asleep, tired from the travel.

"Mommy, I'm not a baby and want to play with the other kids in the water," Junie said. "Remember, you and daddy don't need to come with me, because I can swim now."

"OK, sweetie. Go play. You're too antsy."

Dub stood for a moment, enjoying his boy gleefully romping. He got Mae and the babies settled on the blanket, then walked to the lakeshore where Junie played with a neighbor's child.

"See, Daddy?" He swam back and forth several yards, racing his friend in a couple of feet of water.

"Hey, Dub. Our sons are once again competing for speed just like they race between our houses," Sam said.

Dub turned from Junie to wave at Sam.

"Hey. You're right. Speaking of racing, how's the broccoli you planted?"

The men engaged in competing narratives about the successes of their gardens.

Sam's son returned to sit by his father's side to finish a sandcastle.

Junie sat at the lake's edge, bouncing a small rubber ball in the water. The harder he lobbed it, the farther away it landed in the lake. He caught sight of a white child on the other side of the lake, skipping rocks into the water. They hit the blue surface and hopped along the top like small frogs, closer to Junie each time. He waved at the boy. The boy gestured back. He held up his ball for the boy to see and beckoned him with his arm to come over. The boy shook his head no, then summoned Junie.

Using the instruction learned from his father, Junie stood gingerly, glided into the water, and commenced moving his arms like windmills and kicking his feet rhythmically. He quickly and easily propelled away from where his father had left him.

Pausing to look back at his progress, he tried to stand. His arms grabbed at the water, but it failed to provide security. He stroked the water harder. His feet no longer paddled with vigor but instead wanted to help him run back to shore, but no floor existed to support his feet. Each time his legs extended downward searching for a hard surface, his face sank under the water.

The boy on the other side of the lake beckoned Junie by waving with both arms. Junie reached out to the child. He was too far away to hear the child's instructions.

"Dad, help him! Please help him! He's not there anymore!" said the boy.

The boy's father turned and saw a little brown child bobbing up and down.

"Gregory. We can't help that boy, and don't you bother with him," the man said.

Again, Junie held his hand out to the boy, and at the same time, a tall glass of water poured down his throat. He could not spit it out. Exhausted from the fight, surrender came easily. No longer seeing the white boy or the father, or hearing people laughing and children playing, he focused on the lake's underside with the sun's translucent glow of gold. Eventually the reflection disappeared.

While Dub was talking to Sam, Gregory's voice grew louder in the distance, along with other children playing, but Dub could not understand the words. The sound came from the other side.

When Gregory's father witnessed Junie go under for the last time, he yelled across the distance.

Many bystanders heard a man's voice call, "You people over there, somebody's kid just went under the water."

Mae looked in the direction of the voice, receiving each word. The father took Gregory's hand, walked back to his group, and stood to look at Dub and Sam.

"Junie!" Mae ran along the shore looking at the face of each child. "Where's my baby?"

Dub and Sam clearly caught the father's words, "Kid just went under the water."

When Dub turned to scope out the lake, he caught the father's eyes looking directly at him. Sam looked down where he last saw his own son, comforted to see him placing rocks around the sandcastle.

After a few seconds, Gregory's father said loudly to no one in particular, "What derelicts. They always let their kids run wild." He shook his head all the way back to the blanket where his wife sat waiting with a spread of food like they were at a movie theater ready for the scene to unfold and climax.

Adults picked toddlers out of the lake and placed them on the sand with their families.

Gregory continued to look and point his finger where Junie disappeared. Mae's voice projected above all else.

"Dub! Didn't you watch him? You lost him!" She ran toward the lake.

Unable to swim, Mae desperately waded, flailing her hands beneath the water to grasp hold of her son. Each time, her hands came up empty. Junie no longer frolicked in the water with the other children.

"I'll find our baby," Dub said with determination, scouring the lake's edge.

Sam held on to Mae's waist, pulling her out of the water.

Dub threw off his shoes and dove into the Lake, swimming hard and fast across the distance to the spot where the little boy's finger pointed. He descended under the water, making his eyes open against the sting of sand particles. Fanning his arms deep beneath the surface, he hoped to touch any part of the child's body, until he was forced to come up for air. Shooting upward, he inhaled a lungful and dove repeatedly, coming up empty handed each time and more exhausted after the descent.

Sam beckoned his wife to stay with Mae and jogged into the lake toward his friend. On Dub's return to the surface, he felt Sam lock an arm around his back and pull him to shallow water.

Kneeling in the water and looking across the lake, Dub once again fixed his eyes on Gregory's father. He surged forward, reaching to grab the face that last saw his child.

"You bastard, you watched my son beg for help and didn't even try to save him? I'm going to kill you!"

The father waved an arm at Dub, dismissing the outraged voice and incoherent words.

"Some men went to find a boat to go out into the water and search," Sam said. "Just hold on man, I'm here with you and Mae. Ignore them folks over there. They won't do anything for you but cause you more trouble. Hang on, let's take the fishing boat out. It'll be here soon."

Even after help arrived, nothing could be done. Gregory, his father, and his mother sat on the other side as spectators while two other men dredged the bottom of the lake with long poles and nets, searching for Junie.

When the men located the body not far from where Gregory had pointed, his father nodded in Dub's direction, then retrieved his picnic basket. The mother folded the blanket, and the entire group of onlookers filed out now that the show was over.

Mae's knees weakened and her body collapsed as the rescuers recovered her son's lifeless body. Neighbors picked her up and carried her back to shore. Sobbing, Dub placed Junie in

Mae's arms as she sat in the sand. She buried her face in his neck, pleading for him to come back.

The young family had embarked upon an idyllic day with four children and returned home with three, dropping the fourth off at the funeral home along the way.

CHAPTER 7

TIMOTHY AND KATE (1923–1924)

Tim's work as a butler's assistant for the Benson family proved steady over eight years. Meanwhile, the volatility of life with Betsey as well as Tim's nighttime voyeuristic excursions to the house on Jackson Street continued.

On a warm spring evening Betsey and sixteen-year-old Tim sat alone in the kitchen, finishing slices of ham, beans, and bread. Zeke arrived after work, ate quickly, dropped a coin into the jar, and left to return to his own home for the evening. His brother's desperate pleas failed to encourage Zeke to stay and visit. When Betsey rose from the table, Tim stood up as well to help her clean the kitchen. Neither spoke any words to the other. Betsey looked around the kitchen at the clean sink, the clean floor, the perfectly stacked dishes, and the empty table, then walked out to the porch.

From the serenity in the air came the persistent cry of a baby and then sudden silence. Replaced by a barking dog and immediate quiet after the open and close of a screen door. Then crickets chirped. Betsey wrapped her arms around her shoulders and rocked side to side.

"Um, um, um," she chuckled, leaning over to retrieve a bottle of alcohol from beneath the stoop. Staring at the sky, she sat on the steps, grasping the liquor as if in prayer.

The appearance of the liquor bottle signaled the end of the ritual and the beginning of uncertainty. Tim turned and quietly walked out the front door toward the direction of Upper Orchard.

The olive-skinned girl with long, flowing black curly hair had blossomed since Tim's first visit. The far-reaching branches and expansive trunk of the walnut tree on the home's estate provided him cover for hours. As usual, undetected from behind the tree, on this night he peered directly into the house's parlor, no more than twenty-five feet away, at the adults drinking cordials.

Tim said in a whisper, "Where is she? She must not be home tonight."

A high-pitched but quiet voice said, "Who are you?"

Tim jumped to his feet, wiped his eyes, and rubbed his hands on his pants nervously, taking a step back.

"Who are you?" she asked again.

"Tim, ma'am."

"My name is Kathleen Russo, but call me Kate. I've seen you out the window and glimpse you sometimes when I sneak out of the house. I spy on you too while I smoke in my tree house over there and write in my diary."

Yards from the broad walnut tree that Tim frequented on the Russos' estate stood its twin. The second tree held two distinct differences. A tree hollow near the base of the trunk offered opportunities for animals to hide and for Kate to place a cigar box containing items forbidden by her parents. And nestled in the long thick branches sat a tree house.

Constructed to resemble a dollhouse painted pink with white

trim, the ceiling of the miniature home extended high enough for a young child under five feet to stand. Flower boxes planted with real seasonal flowers dotted windows on each side. Inside, an oil lamp hung as a chandelier. A Persian rug lay beneath a cot covered with a pink floral wool blanket. The cot offered a view of the night sky. Pictures of horses and dolls dotted the wall. A small desk and chair with paper and writing utensils as well as Kate's diary sat beneath a window that framed the distant walnut tree where Tim spent time watching the Russos.

"Watching you is amusing. Where are you from, Tim?"

The girl stood in front of him. The night sky and stars disappeared and all that existed was Kate. She smiled and flicked ashes from the cigarette attached to a long-stemmed holder in her hand. White smoke from the burning paper and tobacco floated between them into Tim's face.

He coughed and covered his mouth. "Excuse me," he said. "I live over in Low Orchard, ma'am. I don't mean any harm."

"I don't think you want to hurt me. Like I said, you've been out here for a long time. I just now decided to see the world from your vantage point. I already write in my diary about seeing you. You must tell me what fascinates you and keeps you coming back."

"I apologize. I'll stop. Please don't turn me in to the police."

"Never. You'd be jailed or even killed if I told anyone. Do you do this at other houses in my neighborhood?"

"I used to, but I found yours the most interesting. I learned so much about living from your family. The others were boring, and just sat and looked at each other. Yours did things with their lives besides perch in a parlor like peacocks and look rich."

Kate laughed. She turned toward the window to quietly observe her family, slowly raised the cigarette holder to her lips, and drew in the vapor. Her rose-colored cheeks slightly sunk in with each inhalation. After each draw, her arm dropped, and then the smoke released through pursed lips. Tim followed the path of the smoke drifting into the darkness. Kate turned to Tim and smiled once more.

"I work as a butler's assistant at the Bensons'," he said, breaking the silence. "They live in the big house on Oak Street."

"Of course. That place is the largest house in town. Janie, the girl that lives there, is my age and doesn't like me much. She has her nose in the air. I'm acquainted with most of these families. They're all stick-in-the-mud types."

"Oh, I learned a lot about this neighborhood from working at the Benson estate. The staff and visitors talk about who dates who, people cheating on other people, who snubs who when party invitations are sent out, who is losing money, and things like that."

"Do they talk about me?"

"I would never say, because that could mean my job, so please don't ask. Just like I'll never talk about meeting you."

He described other homes he spied on and studied, and Kate told him about the family and helped give context to his window observations.

***

As the months moved on, the two young people became friends. They kept the friendship secret and had regular visits at least two nights each week. Monday nights, when Kate's parents played bridge at a friend's house, and on Wednesdays, when her parents went to prayer meetings at their church, with few exceptions. Other times, Tim tried to stop by after working at the Bensons' home. He brought homework from school, and with Kate's help, he became top of his class. They alternated their meetings between the tree house and the gardeners' storage shed, using dim lanterns for light.

As their friendship grew, the pair spent time in the tree house during temperate weather.

Tim learned a great deal from Kate and Kate learned less about Tim. Sitting in the quiet of the tree house doing homework, Tim stared pensively into the distance.

"What's wrong?" Kate asked.

"I am reading about the Civil War."

"I heard my dad say he would have more workers at his factory and pay less in wages if slaves were around still."

"That means I would be a slave."

"Oh, I wasn't talking about you, Tim. I wouldn't want you to be a slave. You don't look like a slave."

"My dad was born a slave. Before I came to Morriston we lived on a plantation, but we weren't slaves."

"Wow! How could you be on a plantation the way you look? What was it like on a plantation? From the pictures I've seen in schoolbooks, slaves look happy, singing songs, and the owners gave you a house."

Tim looked down at his schoolbook and the picture of the brown enslaved woman with a scarf wrapped around her hair, holding a white child in her lap. Turning the page, he saw a picture of a brown man hanging from a noose and two white men holding rifles.

"Why do you look sad?" Kate said.

"Ah, nothing." Tim abruptly closed the book. "What are you reading?" he said, straining to smile.

"My teacher shared some papers with me about the Nineteenth Amendment of the Constitution. Although the amendment says women cannot be kept from voting, some states still make it hard for women to vote. Men try to keep us submissive and almost invisible in society."

"Same with Negroes," Tim murmured quietly.

"What?"

Tim shook his head. "Nothing."

"My teacher belongs to a suffrage movement. These ladies are asking the federal government to erect a monument honoring Black servants who take care of white babies. Isn't that wonderful? I have a mammie, Sadie, who has taken care of me since I was born. I adore her, sometimes even more than my own mother."

Tim looked at the history book again, picked it up, and packed it in a bag with other school materials. He adjusted his position, putting more distance between himself and Kate, and folded his arms. Kate continued reading silently while Tim sat looking around the small room.

"Your mother seems nice when I see her through the window," he finally said after several minutes.

"Yes, but I don't want to be her. I want to be free to do as I please. She's a grown woman and my dad still tells her what to do." Kate's forehead furrowed. She reached for the cigar box and took out a cigarette, placed it in a holder and put the holder between pursed lips. Handing a book of matches to Tim, he automatically lit her cigarette. Kate inhaled deeply and blew out a large cloud of smoke.

"But you are free. Look at you. Look around you." Tim immediately rose and grabbed his book bag. "Not like me," Tim muttered.

"Tim, you must speak up," Kate said before taking another drag from the cigarette. "Anyway, let's stop for the night. I have an English paper due tomorrow. My mom also told me she wants to go over some social engagements that I need to attend with them. Ugh. I hate the phoniness of it all."

***

Several days later at the Bensons', classical music played softly on the record player in the drawing room after dinner. A bell rang in the kitchen. Tim swiftly pulled on his white gloves. Without a sound when his shoes met the tile, and barely breathing, he arrived to pick up the last of the cocktail glasses, placing them on the silver tray. Janie kissed her parents on the cheek, then ran up the curved staircase to retire in her bedroom.

"Timothy, we will need you tomorrow, Friday, until quite late," Mrs. Benson said. "Guests are coming for dinner. No need to put on your best tailcoat."

"Yes, ma'am."

"Charles," she said, "I'm still not certain about this family. Janie told me today that they're social climbers. They're rather dark. I don't think they're Southerners. Perhaps Mediterranean, you think?"

"Oh, lovey," Mr. Benson said with a pipe clenched between his teeth. "We just need to be careful. But the husband could be an investor in my new mill, so I'm willing to invite him for dinner, but we won't open the best Scotch for him."

"Janie said their daughter, Kate, is quite attractive but rather strange. A little worldly. We must not let the girls visit alone. I will insist that Kate joins the adult women in the parlor after the meal. If she is worldly that way, I don't want our Janie learning things she shouldn't."

"All the more reason to feed them quickly, then I'll befriend the husband for an investment."

"I won't feel obligated to invite the wife to any of my clubs or social circles."

"Tim, why are you standing there staring at us with the crystal? Do your job, boy," Mr. Benson said.

Mr. Benson folded the newspaper. Tim approached him, ritually held out the tray for the newspaper's disposal. He then laid the tray on a serving table and retrieved the crystal ashtray. Returning to Mr. Benson, Tim held the ashtray with both hands. Mr. Benson unclenched his teeth to remove the pipe and dump the ashes in the ashtray. Tim placed the ashtray next to the newspaper and glasses.

He brought Mrs. Benson a sheer cotton fabric to cover her needlework stand and carefully packed the equipment in a sewing box. The couple stood, nodded to each other, and Mrs. Benson led the procession through the foyer and up the stairs. The husband and wife entered their separate suites, closing the doors for the evening. Tim stood next to the serving table until the locks latched. He swiftly turned off the drawing room lights, picked up the tray, and scurried out of the parlor and into the kitchen where he handed the glasses to the maid.

Tim exhaled loudly, collapsing his shoulders. He finally spoke.

"Mr. Larry, who is coming for dinner tomorrow?" he asked the senior butler.

"Mr. Russo, his wife, and daughter. Sadie is his daughter Kate's nanny. Sadie's my girl. We're getting married, or may marry if she accepts my proposal."

"Mrs. Benson expects me to work late Friday night. Do I have to?"

"Of course. You aren't thinking of skipping? I'll fire you before you walk out of here."

"All right. I'll be here."

He, Mr. Larry, and the maid finished cleaning, and everyone returned to their homes except for Mr. Larry, who slept in the butler's quarters behind the kitchen.

***

The next evening, the church bells rang five times. Betsey rose slowly from the steps, bracing herself on the porch post.

"Tim. Tim. What's taking you so long? You usually go to work by now. Don't be late and lose that job. It pays too much."

Tim appeared in the kitchen in a white starched shirt and black pressed suit. He wiped the black shoe polish from his hands with a cotton cloth while staring at his shoes.

"Hold your head up, boy. What's wrong with you?"

"Nothing."

Tim scowled and turned away from Betsey, who was wearing one of the two floral housedresses she'd made years ago at the plantation. Stains from many spills of liquor blended with the patterns of the dress.

Tim steadily moved around the room, disposing of the blackened rag, straightening his bow tie, brushing lint from his jacket, then smoothing back his dark wavy hair.

"Look at you, looking like a Hatch." Water rose in her bloodshot eyes. "I used to be pretty. Master Hatch said he liked us mulatto women." Betsey's sadness quickly turned to anger. "Don't let them women in Upper Orchard put their hands on you. Now you're seventeen, growing taller with them muscles, they're really going to try to seduce you. You'll never be the same once they get what they want, and their men will lynch you if they find out. That's what they do if a colored man touches a white woman."

Tim paused, opening the back door. "Yes, ma'am."

At the Bensons', Tim's hands shook the moment Mr. Larry said, "I must answer the front door."

Footsteps. Loud ones, soft ones, heavy ones, and the slight clicking of high heels drew closer to the kitchen and then faded into the parlor. Men's and women's voices blended. Tim stood behind the dining room door with the silver tray in his hand.

Fast, rhythmic steps approached, and a hand pushed the door, which just missed Tim's chest.

"Walk in there, kid, and get the beverage requests. Mrs. Benson's expecting you."

Nodding at Larry, Tim pulled the front of his suit and marched into the parlor. *Just be invisible,* he told himself, approaching the broad arched entrance.

"Ah. Here he is. Timothy, everyone will take a glass of iced tea."

After bowing to Mrs. Benson, Tim immediately spun around and retreated to the kitchen.

Upon his return, Kate's gaze followed Tim as he advanced

down the hall with a straight back, chin lifted, steadily holding the tray of beverages. One white-gloved hand on its side while the tray was balanced on the palm of his other gloved hand. With great precision, he served the glasses one at a time, and spoke to no one. He kept his eyes down and he nodded as each guest successfully removed their glass.

The guests alternated between mesmerized, chuckling, and feigning stoicism in their own conversations, oblivious to the world around them. Tim circled the room methodically. As he came closer and closer to Kate, he never took his eyes off the crystal, ensuring that each guest's hand clutched the glass.

Kate took a deep breath, flexing her hands, which were also covered with white gloves. When he got to her, Tim bowed slightly, observing the balance of the silver tray in one hand and the final remaining glass on top.

"Ma'am," he whispered.

"Thank you," she murmured.

Janie, standing next to Kate, scowled.

"Kate, you don't talk to the help. You certainly never thank them. And he shouldn't say anything to you."

"Sorry, Janie," Kate said, lowering her eyes.

Tim quickly glanced up at Janie, and unflinching, completed his work.

The dinner service proceeded similarly. Between each course, Tim sat in the kitchen on a stool, nervously playing with his fingers and awaiting instructions from the cook or Mr. Larry. When they called his name, he jumped as if it were an unexpected event.

From the foyer, after dessert and cordials, voices grew louder as goodbyes were exchanged and footsteps headed to the front door. Larry's booming voice echoed: "Yes, sir." "Your hat, sir." "Let me help, sir."

Tim sat at the kitchen table mindlessly wiping down the crystal, porcelain, and silver for the maid to store for the next day.

"Boy."

Tim startled and his hands shook when he saw Larry leaning toward him.

"Didn't you hear me calling you? Go serve another Scotch to Mr. Benson. Now."

"She was a lovely girl," Mrs. Benson said, "and rather exotic looking with her dark skin. Her mother is practically white. Strange thing, Italians come in different colors. Did you notice, Mr. Benson? Kate looks more like her father. I hope she didn't talk trashy to Janie. I carefully monitored the girls' conversations."

"The father's clothing manufacturing business is doing very well. He buys more and more from the textile plant and says their biggest products are socks and men's underwear. They are selling like gangbusters. Can you believe that? He must be pulling in the cash. I need to be careful because they'll never really shine to him in the social circles. His accent is too heavy. Gives off a foxy air, but I'll be just nice enough to secure his investment in the company. You too, lovey. I need you to be nice."

Tim circled the room, served the Scotch, picked up the used glasses, and softly exited the parlor.

After the long evening at the Bensons', Tim returned home, where Betsey moved slowly around the kitchen, heating up his dinner.

"Hey, Mama," he said, loosening his bow tie, then waiting. After several seconds passed without response, Tim turned toward the back door, hands in his pockets. Dropping his head, he approached the porch and sat down on the steps in the same spot Betsey parked herself between house chores. The quart of whiskey that regularly kept her company lay at his feet. Tim lowered his head to his hands and shook it.

"Invisible. I'll always be invisible. It's too hard. Kate showed me I can do more."

Reaching down, he lifted the bottle, quickly glanced behind

him into the kitchen, then up and down the row of backyards. He took a swig of the hard liquor, swallowing it with ease. A second, much larger swallow poured down his throat and he sighed. The negative feelings seemed to leave his body. He sat back with his elbows resting on the wooden planks of the porch, bottle in hand. Betsey's humming stopped and footsteps approached behind Tim. He quickly put the bottle back in its place.

After eating, Tim took off his butler's uniform and put on a fresh cotton shirt and brown pants. He jogged across the railroad tracks, then passed through the business district and into the world he increasingly longed for. A place much different from his own, with brick-paved streets, floral bushes lining the front of homes, and opulent facades. With darkness surrounding the neighborhood, families sat tucked inside their parlors, visiting.

The tree house awaited his arrival; the cigar box shoved in the hollow of the walnut tree became their way of leaving messages to each other. The box held a piece of paper. The smell of tobacco rose from the container and the words *See you tomorrow night in the tree house* drifted off the page. He gently closed the box that also held the cigarette, a lighter, and a long-stemmed holder as evidence of a forbidden part of Kate's life.

His gait became more hesitant the closer he came to view the house nestled in the branches. In the distance sat Kate and her family. Tears rose in his eyes as he observed the family in front of the fireplace while a butler entered the room to serve a nightcap. Tim turned and ran, not stopping until he arrived home. He ran past Betsey sitting on the porch, the bottle of soothing elixir turned up to her lips. With no other outlet than Upper Orchard, he threw himself on his bed face down, screaming into the pillow, releasing his emotions.

The next evening after work, instead of meeting Kate in the tree house as she requested, Tim stealthily ambled around Upper Orchard, peering into homes until he found appealing entertainment—the lure to houses where men played poker well into the night, drinking liquor, gambling, and smoking cigars.

Filled with excitement and curiosity, the following week he shorted the wages placed in Betsey's jar to buy his own playing cards and Scotch. Night after night he scoured the neighborhood for poker games. Upon finding one, he peered through the window, and with his own cards, played whoever's hand he could see inside.

Kate checked the cigar box each day for his response to her note. After two weeks with no response, she decided to walk around the neighborhood instead of sitting in the tree house writing in her diary and smoking. She found Tim crouched in the front bushes of a home up the street, watching men at a card table. A notebook and pencil lay on the ground, cards were splayed in his hand, and a bottle of Scotch was tucked in his pocket.

"What are you doing?"

Tim jumped.

"I've missed you. Is this what you've been doing?"

He put his fingers to his lips.

She crouched down next to him and leaned her head on his shoulder, touching him for the first time. Tim turned briefly to look at the top of her head, gave a slight one-sided smile, and allowed his cheek to brush against her hair. Neither mentioned the dinner at the Bensons' house two weeks prior.

CHAPTER 8

BETSEY'S WRATH (1924)

When he returned home later that evening, Betsey sat parked at the kitchen table, moving coins around the flat wooden surface, counting them over and over. She jerked her head toward the back porch when Tim sauntered up the steps.

"Tim, why are you putting less money in the jar?"

"Mr. Coats hasn't been giving me many grocery delivery runs. My tips are down."

She glared at him as he opened the screen door, then released it to slam behind him.

"Look at me in my eyes when I talk to you."

"Mama, I'm not lying." He slowly dragged his feet to the icebox and yanked it open to pull out the last bit of meatloaf.

"The money jar is steadily emptying. I count those coins every day."

"To do what? Buy liquor and get sloppy drunk?"

Betsey darted from the table, reached for the broom handle, and swung it directly into Tim's stomach. He bent over, gasping for air. The plate and food splattered across the kitchen floor. She struck him with a second blow across his back. His knees collapsed under him. Repeated blows landed along his legs and buttocks. Tim lay still, arms covering his face and head, absorbing pain until the strikes slowed.

"I can't do this anymore." She lost the stamina to raise her arms. Her face drenched in tears, eyes red and breath wheezing, she bent over with her hands on her knees.

Silence filled the air; neither moved from the place of torture, refusing to see the other. A train's horn blew. A dog barked persistently.

"Y'all all right over there?" A woman's voice called from the porch next door.

Enduring the pool of sweat stinging the welts that broke through his skin, Tim snarled, "This is the last time you'll beat me. This isn't Green Creek. I deserve better."

Betsey threw the broom at the air that carried his words and staggered to her bedroom.

Tim struggled to stand, then retreated to his room, locking the door. The newest bruises throbbed beneath his shirt. Not even cold water from the basin alleviated the pain in his face. Fully dressed, he lay down on the bed, crawled between the sheet and blanket, and folded into a fetal position. His entire body covered, he lay awake, immobile, until the following morning, when sounds of someone rummaging in the kitchen broke the paralysis.

Tim slowly unlatched the door and cracked it several inches to see Zeke holding the broom, sweeping up particles of meatloaf and the broken plate. Tim reluctantly entered the hallway to watch Zeke throw the debris into a garbage can, move the table and chair to their proper places, and return the kitchen to its normally clean state. Glimpsing Tim, Zeke chuckled. From the icebox, Zeke removed eggs, bacon, and bread and silently made breakfast for them both.

Over a glass of milk, Zeke said, "Another bad night with Mama, huh?"

Tim nodded.

Zeke inspected the splotches of black-and-blue marks on Tim's face and arms and returned to his food. He informed Tim of his upcoming move to take a coal mining job in West Virginia and his sudden marriage. Tim implored him to stay in Morriston.

"Zeke, how can you leave Mama?"

"Easy. I don't live in her house. I eat, leave money in the jar for the food, and return to my own life. We all came here together from Green Creek. But I decided that losing my sanity, and being something I'm not, aren't a part of my life. I find peace where I can."

The brothers ate in silence. Zeke left for work and Tim went to school.

Two days later, Zeke left Morriston, and during those two days, Betsey stayed in the house shut in her bedroom.

Tim resumed visits to the Russo estate, and when Kate could not meet in the tree house or gardeners' shed, he watched card games through Upper Orchard windows.

***

Thunder and lightning consumed the day of Kate's seventeenth birthday. Tim arrived at the estate and checked the cigar box in the tree hollow, then ran to the gardeners' shed. As a gift, he presented her with a white lace crocheted handkerchief bought at the general store. That evening, their relationship grew more intimate, in the sense that the conversations revealed their life goals, their happiness and disappointments, and their challenges at school and with Kate's family. They sat shoulder to shoulder and leg to leg, but nothing more.

"Tim, let's go to your neighborhood tonight."

"Why?"

"I want to see if you live as poorly as people say."

Tim withdrew and turned to look directly at Kate.

"Who says Low Orchard is poor?"

"Everybody. My family, my classmates, and friends," Kate said in a matter-of-fact tone.

"Not true." Tim scowled and elevated his voice and shook his head fervently several times.

"So take me to your house."

"No." Tim stood up, waving his arms, and then pointed at Kate. "You don't belong there just like I don't really belong here."

"But you are here," Kate said, raising her voice too. "You came here. Why?" Kate sat up on her knees and leaned toward Tim.

"I told you why. And don't you ever try to find my house either," Tim growled. He abruptly turned away from Kate, hit the wall with his fist, bolted through the shed door, and slammed it shut. He ran home without stopping in the torrential rain.

A week went by with no contact between the friends. Tim wrote a one-sentence note to place in the cigar box. *Kate, I apologize for my rude behavior and hope you will forgive me. Tim.* Tim removed the box from the tree hollow, and upon opening it, he saw a sealed envelope. He set the box on the ground and walked with the envelope to his usual walnut tree, where he read from the glow of lights around the home.

Tim, I am sorry my words upset you. I want to know you better as you know me. But I am willing to do it in your own time. I will be in the tree house on our regular days should you decide to return. Your friend Kate.

Tim walked back to the tree hollow and returned the box to its hiding place, then climbed the ladder to the tree house, where Kate sat waiting. They smiled at each other, recommencing their visits.

***

One late spring evening, after doing homework in the tree house, Kate grew silent.

"What's wrong?" Tim asked.

"When I graduate in a month, my parents are sending me to Vassar College." Tears rose in her eyes.

Tim turned to sit facing Kate with a quizzical look. "What is Vassar College?"

"A place for women to continue their education and become teachers or nurses, or be trained for some other profession."

"I've never heard of a college, and I don't think I know anyone who has been to one. Maybe my teachers went to college, I guess."

He sat staring at Kate, leaning toward her face, yet not touching her. Kate stuttered, trying to release the words. The tears finally rolled down her cheeks. The more she struggled, the closer Tim drew, until he held her hand.

She finally blurted out, "My parents really want me to meet and marry a wealthy, educated man from Yale University who can offer me this same lifestyle or even improve my standing in society."

"What is Yale University?"

"It's a prestigious place that men attend to become doctors, lawyers, or successful businessmen. They usually come from well-to-do families," she explained, her tone becoming apologetic. She shrugged her shoulders and cocked her head to the side. "I'm sorry."

Tim looked at the pictures on the tree house wall as if he were bidding them goodbye. He turned to look at the full moon through the window near the cot. The diary sitting on the desk drew his attention.

Finally, in a conceding manner, he said, "I never thought about your leaving Morriston."

"I'll miss you. But I'll return for holidays and summer break, unless I travel abroad, as many students do to expand their knowledge. I may go to countries throughout Europe and study art or archeology. Won't that be exciting? I can bring back souvenirs and send you letters from all over the world."

Tim continued to stare at Kate's face and the glow in her eyes from the lantern.

"I'll miss you too." He turned to face the tree house door.

She stopped talking, leaned over, and kissed him on the cheek. He pulled back with a startled look.

"We can kiss," she said. "This is what people do when they're attracted to each other."

"Really?"

Kate reached out, and that was the moment the relationship changed to include intimacy in a way Tim had never experienced before. She guided his hands to release the buttons on her clothes and directed his fingers to remove her underwear and then his own. She whispered instructions in his ear. The words roused his body instinctively to engage with hers. A new world opened for him.

Returning to his house, he walked in the front door. Looking through to the back porch, he saw Betsey on the steps, head leaning against the post.

"I need an exodus," Tim said quietly to himself, observing the paint peeling from the exterior wood.

The next day, he went early to school: a wood-frame single-floor building, painted white with black trim, a steeple and bell on top, sitting on the property of one of two churches in Low Orchard. Five large rooms made up the entirety of Saint John's High School. Four of the school rooms housed one grade each, ninth through twelfth. The other large room combined a library, lunchroom, and recreation hall. Behind the building a small duplex cabin housed living quarters for teachers.

When Tim arrived, the doors were open but no students

occupied the hallway. "Principal" labeled a small room near the front, and a sliver of light emerged from under the door. He knocked timidly. Mr. Thomas beckoned him to come inside.

"Hello, Tim. My, you're early. What can I do for you?" Mr. Thomas said, hanging up his jacket on a hook. He sat down at his desk. Tim was still standing; Mr. Thomas gestured toward the chair in front.

Tim sat. "How do I attend a college? Did you go?"

"Wow. You got straight to the point. Well, I did," Mr. Thomas said. "I graduated from Talladega College right here in Alabama. There are other places where we Negroes mostly attend."

"But I want to go to Yale, sir."

"That's over one thousand miles away in Connecticut. What would your mama do if you moved that far away?"

"She wouldn't be happy because I couldn't send her money."

Mr. Thomas raised his eyebrows. "Well, Yale wouldn't take you, or me for that matter, and I already earned a degree. You're lucky that this school is unique and prepares students for college. You may not realize that Saint John's was built the year before you started because of money from the church and a Jewish philanthropist that assured you had a four-year high school experience with a full academic curriculum of English, science, math, and history. Otherwise, because of the segregated school system in Alabama, and meager funding for schools generally, your education would have stopped at eighth grade at the highest. Most of Alabama's government funds for education go to support white students. For us Negroes, we have enough government money and facilities to hold school maybe three days a week."

Tim sat pensively. "That's what happened with my older brothers and sisters. But you haven't said how the admission works for college."

"You did well this year in your studies, so let's begin by

talking to the people at Talladega. And, if you do well your first and second years, then maybe the people at Talladega could help you approach Yale."

"How soon could I start?" Tim sat on the edge of his chair, leaning toward Mr. Thomas's desk.

"You must request admission."

Tim sat back and slumped in the chair.

Mr. Thomas quickly said, wagging his finger at Tim, "But, I'll mail a letter and ask if you can begin after the summer. If you're admitted, you'll be the first pupil from this school to attend college. I believe you can be successful."

***

It only took until July, when Mr. Thomas went to the grocery store and handed Tim a letter. He'd secured Tim a spot at Talladega, not far from Morriston.

Two hours later, Betsey was standing at the basin, washing dishes, when Tim guardedly walked into the kitchen. An apple pie sat in the middle of the table, freshly out of the oven. A breeze carried the fragrance out the back door to share with the neighborhood. He took in the serene scene with a small smile on his face. Betsey's hair was braided down her back, and her housedress was clean and ironed. She hummed a joyous tune.

"Mama."

She continued to hum, head down, scrubbing burnt food from the bottom of a cast-iron skillet.

Tim cleared his throat, still standing in the threshold between the kitchen and living room.

"Mama," he said a little louder.

Startled, she quickly turned her head.

"Oh, Tim, I didn't hear you walk in. I thought you would've been at your grocery store or houseboy job."

"I'm on my way to the Bensons', but I wanted to tell you something first. Can we talk?"

"Why don't we do that while I pour you a bowl of bean soup with neck bones."

"Sure."

Betsey turned to retrieve a bowl from the cabinet. She opened the pot and a trail of smoke rose, carrying the aroma of pork throughout the kitchen. She reached the ladle down and scooped up a large piece of meat surrounded by beans. After repeating the process until the bowl was filled to the brim, she gingerly shuffled to the table, avoiding any spillage on the clean floor.

"Thanks," Tim said, standing nervously and shuffling his feet side to side. "I got news from the school today. The principal, Mr. Thomas, got me into Talladega College. People go there for more learning and to become teachers, doctors, and nurses and such."

"Yes, I'm not illiterate. They've talked about those colored colleges in church. Talladega is in Alabama. Not too far from here."

Betsey returned to the cabinet, swiftly opened a drawer, slammed it shut, and returned with a spoon and cloth napkin and laid them firmly on the table. Without looking at Tim she then stomped back to the sink to continue scrubbing the skillet.

"By the way, you can't go. Now sit down and eat," she said without taking her eyes off the dirty water in the sink.

"Why not, Mama?"

"We need you to work and we can't afford it. It costs money. I said sit down and eat."

The water in the sink splashed around as Betsey scrubbed the dishes more vigorously.

"Mr. Thomas found me a job at the college to pay for school and my room. I'll go to class for eight hours, work at the library for eight hours, where I can do my homework at the same time, and still sleep eight hours at night."

"Boy, I can't listen to this mess. Just sit down and eat."

"No, I won't sit down. Not yet."

Betsey spun around to look directly at Tim. Every muscle in her face tensed and her eyes squinted as she grasped the brush in one hand and the skillet in the other. Tim took a step closer to the hallway leading to the bedrooms.

"What would I do for money? Most of your brothers and sisters don't give a damn about me. You and Zeke are different. I can't keep up this house without help from you boys. Zeke sends me a little money since he eloped and moved to West Virginia with the girl at the bar, Zelda. I wouldn't be surprised if she's pregnant. And forget about Dub, especially after poor Junie died, God rest his little soul. Tragic. Mae keeps track of each penny Dub makes and keeps it for her uppity self. What she needs is to stop having babies. I should know."

Tim raised his voice and flailed his arms.

"Take in someone to rent my bedroom." He pulled several coins from his pocket and threw them on the floor. "I don't care. I gotta leave Morriston. I'm stifled. I thought it would make you proud to have a son going to college to make something of himself. I could be a doctor. You can't move past being a slave. If I stay here, that's all we'll ever be: invisible servants."

The room went silent. The fingers on Betsey's hands spread apart. A sudden boom reverberated from the wooden floor when the scrub brush dropped from her right and the skillet from her left.

"Who the hell do you think you're talking to, you ingrate!" She glared at Tim and screamed, "Your daddy and I risked our lives traveling to this town. Now all of you kids think you're too good to be here and leave me here to rot. Dub and Mae make sure they aren't seen with me. She's busy trying to impress people when she's a nothing like the rest of us."

Tears burst from Tim's eyes, his face turned red, and sweat beaded on his forehead. "You're doing it to yourself with all the drinking, Mama. Today is the first time in a long time I've seen you sober and in clean clothes. Most of the time you're an embarrassment. Even the church women talk about you."

Betsey took one step toward Tim, leaned in, and said, "Get out of my face. Now!"

"If I attend Yale, I can make tons of money after graduation," he wailed, clasping his hands together as if in prayer. Spit ran from his mouth. Mucous from his nose combined with the flowing tears.

"I said get out of my face."

Tim knocked the bowl of soup off the table, stormed into his bedroom to grab his butler's uniform, and ran to the Bensons' to work.

The application to Talladega remained a secret from Kate until Tim was accepted. The next day, a hot July night, they met in the tree house after her parents left for a bridge party.

"Look at this," he said, handing her the letter addressed to Mr. Thomas. "I'm going to college too."

She silently read the letter, then raised her nose up at Tim and said, "I never heard of Talladega. Is that a colored place? How good is it?"

"My principal got his degree there, so it must be good. And he runs the high school in Low Orchard. He said that if I do well there, Yale may admit me after two years. You at Vassar and me at Yale."

"Maybe. Yale is very selective. If we got together, we'd be forced to live in another country, like France, because we're different. But I don't want to think about negative stuff. Let's talk about happier things that are more realistic."

Kate spent the next hour telling Tim what he needed for Talladega and talking about how she wanted to decorate her room at Vassar.

***

Until her departure for college, their intimate meetings continued in the gardeners' storage shed at the back of the estate, to confine the sounds of their lovemaking. When Kate unbuttoned her blouse, Tim obliged by removing his clothes too.

Two weeks before leaving for Talladega, he left the Bensons' and walked the blocks to the Russos' estate. Since he had not received a note in the walnut tree, Tim arrived at the gardeners' shed at the time they had agreed upon for that night. Lightly knocking on the door as he usually did, he did not hear her voice say, "I'm here." Yet, he eased open the door and peered inside at the wood bench where she typically sat waiting for him. Instead, the cigar box occupied the seat. Stepping inside, the door closed, sealing him alone in a sheltered world only he and Kate knew. Picking up the box, he lifted the top and found a note:

> Tim, our love has produced a child. My parents know I am having a baby, but they do not know you are the father. I cannot meet you anymore. I am being watched every minute and do not want anyone to hurt you. They told the college that I will not start until a year from now due to a severe illness. I cannot stop you from watching me through the window. It may give me some comfort. I will sit in the parlor as much as I can. At some point, my parents will send me away. Your friend, Kate.

Tim froze, clutching the note. Finally peeling his focus from the sheet of paper, he turned around slowly and opened the door. Standing in the threshold, he gazed across the dark acreage toward Kate's home, seeing a small glow emanating from the window of the parlor and a single light upstairs. He stepped outside.

The door closed behind him, shutting out a world where he felt safe. Gravity pulled him down with his back to the door, where he crouched on the ground to bury his head between his knees, grasping the box against his chest like he wanted to embed it in his heart. Silent tears poured down his face.

Hesitantly, he rose and walked near the large walnut tree, lumbering around aimlessly. His feet and hands gravitated to the ladder, taking him up to the tree house he'd visited many times before, but he soon retreated to earth, unable to reenter that world without Kate.

Mindlessly walking back to Low Orchard, the front of Saint John's High School came into view. A lone light glowed in the principal's office. Mr. Thomas's shadow moved behind the window blinds. Inertia glued Tim's feet to the ground. The depth of emotion and shock from the letter's contents further detached him from existence. The cigar box affixed between the palms of his hands, he instinctively climbed the few stairs leading to the front door. Tim saw a hand reach the doorknob and startled when it looked like his own. The "Principal" sign greeted him, and the same familiar hand knocked on the door.

"Sir, may I talk to you a moment?" he heard himself say, opening the door slowly.

"Oh. Tim, you startled me. I didn't expect anyone at this time of night. Come in. I'm making plans for next year. Shouldn't you be prepping for Talladega? Is there a problem?" Mr. Thomas asked.

"Yes. I won't be attending Talladega. Well, I met someone in Upper Orchard, and we became good friends," Tim said. He extended a trembling arm. "She left this for me."

Mr. Thomas took the box and opened it. He saw the cigarette and holder. "I assume you want me to read the letter on top?"

Tim nodded.

After reading the letter, he looked at Tim and shook his

head. "Oh. I'm so sorry. Son, you can't do anything about it now. Under normal circumstances, you should take care of that responsibility. But an Upper Orchard white girl? They will deal with it for you, so you can't let this deprive you of the life you could have otherwise. The best thing to do is forget her, forget the baby, go to Talladega, and move on."

"But those people in Upper Orchard are taking my child and Kate from me. You're telling me I have no voice or choice? I'm tired of being told to stay invisible when it comes to dealing with those people. Is there nothing I can control?"

Mr. Thomas rose from his chair, walked around to the front of his desk, and placed his hand on Tim's shoulder. Tim lowered his head. Tears dropped to the floor.

"Look, Tim, those people are doing what's best for you and that girl," he said in a stern voice. "With some things in this world you have no choice. But you do have control over whether you become successful in your life despite the circumstances. You're a smart young man. Now is the time to use those smarts."

Mr. Thomas studied the young man sitting in despair. He moved back to his desk, facing Tim. Once the crying subsided, Mr. Thomas spoke.

"Tim, look at me. Right here in my eyes."

Tim raised his head, finally reconnecting with himself and the state of his life.

Mr. Thomas said in a soft voice, "Trust me, that girl will move on. Especially if they see a brown baby come out of her. Go to Talladega. Apply to Yale if you still want to, but not because of her. But in any case, finish your degree and keep rising and growing. That you can control if you focus and dedicate yourself."

"I understand," Tim said.

Mr. Thomas returned to his chair.

"Son, the truth is you must prepare to move on without her," Mr. Thomas said, handing the box back to Tim.

CHAPTER 9

CULTIVATING LIFE (1924)

After Junie's death, Dub packed his grief in a lockbox in the dark recesses of his mind where memories of Green Creek and Tuttle's murder resided. All available room in his mind existed only to raise the older children, Matthew, Bernie, and Amaya; bond with one-year-old twins Calvin and Genese; and prepare for a newborn any day.

Mae's grand expectations continued fueling Dub's ambitions at the textile factory, from hauling bales of cotton to a janitorial job to a machine operator's position, a rarity in those days for a Black man. His journey to work began before sunup each morning and led him down the brick streets to the outskirts of town.

Each weekday morning, men formed a line as they approached the wide entryway of the two-story wood-and-brick textile factory. One by one they found their names on punch cards in a slot carved into a wooden board hanging on the wall. Robotically, and in silence, each man removed the paper, slipped it into the time clock to stamp their time of arrival, and returned the card to its slot on the wall. They moved several feet to an open room lined with lockers, found their name, and placed their coats and hats and lunch bags inside. Then they proceeded to a workstation. The movements were ceremonial and procedural.

Dub did not mind the solemnity because it gave him time to think and focus on doing his best work in a place where he typically did not see another brown-skinned person until near the end of the day. All the other Black men worked on the loading docks or the evening shift cleaning equipment and floors. Being that the other workers ostracized him, he learned the other jobs around the factory and came up with a strategy to become the first Black supervisor in the shop.

Lee, another factory worker, lived on the edge of the Upper Orchard community where the white laborers lived. He and Dub chatted each day to pass the time as they each operated spinning machines.

"Dub, did you see the story in the newspaper about some coal mining agents coming to town from a company up north?" Lee asked. "They want men to take the striking workers' jobs. They pay more than any floor job here. Oh, I forgot. Negroes can't read. Are you one that can read?"

Dub stared. "If I wasn't at work and hadn't been around you all these years, I'd hurt you behind that comment. I'm choosing to indulge you by answering the asinine question. I can read. But with five mouths to feed now, buying a newspaper is not on my list of things to spend money on. You're such a—"

"The newspapers are all gone anyway. Ignore I said anything."

After a while, Dub looked up from his machine and said, "I'm interested in the job, though. My brother Zeke just moved to West Virginia with his new pregnant bride. He got a job as a coal loader in some big mine out that way. He told me a lot of people are moving north and the companies provide you with a house. A grocery store is on the grounds for the workers too. Zeke's making more money than in Morriston."

"That company probably wouldn't hire you anyway to work underground. You got no skills."

"You haven't a clue who I am, do you? What the hell makes you think I don't want to leave this small town as much as you?"

It was time.

Morriston summers were all piercing hot sun, humidity, and sticky skin. After punching the clock to leave the textile plant, Dub emerged into the open air on a July afternoon, stopping to raise his face toward the sun's rays.

"Mae, we have a bright future," he said, giving her a kiss on the cheek upon arriving home.

Mae busied herself in their small kitchen as usual, stacking leftover chicken meat between slices of bread. The kitchen had one rectangular wooden table with benches running along either side and a chair at each end. She took pride in her kitchen, stocked with a small icebox, a sink to hold water brought in from the well at the end of the street, and a wood stove and oven.

When Dub came home for lunch, he ate in peace while Matthew and Bernie attended school and the other children took a nap.

"Wash your hands. I have your lunch ready," she said, smiling but never taking her eyes off the task.

Diligent hands promptly placed the chicken sandwich and a glass of water on the table in front of Dub as he sat down in the chair.

"Why is it you never look worn out after taking care of a house full of children and ironing a couple of bags of table linens from the hotel?" he asked, taking a bite of his sandwich. "And you're pregnant again too. Sit down, I need to tell you about this job opportunity in the coal mines up north. This may be the chance we need."

Mae listened intensely as Dub repeated the information from his coworker Lee.

"I want the life Zeke has in West Virginia, and you promised me a house like Miss Clara's. It was big with expensive furniture. But there's something about working in a coal mine that doesn't settle well with me. Digging underground means danger. Being a widow with five, almost six, children is not my goal," she said. "But I guess the risk is worth the money."

"Yes. Isn't Zeke making lots of money? You told me that Zelda's letter went on and on about their beautiful home and how Negroes and white people integrate and are paid the same. Right?"

"Yes. Their letters do make it exciting. I dream of a grand house and fancy dishes. Let's just follow Zeke to West Virginia where you can be certain to make lots of money. Plus, we need to move away from Betsey. The way she stumbles around town is an embarrassment."

"Mae, sometimes you act like your pride is tied to starched clothes, clean children, an impeccable reputation, and a fine house."

"You're right. That's what I want. Well, when are the interviews? Maybe I can help you prepare. If the money is right, I'm sure I can bear the thought of you working beneath the earth in the dark."

"Lee wouldn't tell me when the interviews are taking place. I must find out in a slick sort of way. He obviously doesn't want me there. But I promise to learn all I can about safety."

"What if the job you want goes to other men?"

"Hon, we won't know unless I try. Right? I understand you want to improve the way we live. Let me do some research and learn what this work is all about."

He quickly stuffed the last bits of chicken sandwich in his mouth, washed it down with the water, gave his wife a hug, and waved goodbye, running out the front door to his second job.

Dub walked several blocks from his house to the general store, situated on the edge of downtown and next to Low Orchard, drawing patrons from both communities and all walks of life. He whistled while he traveled the short walk, taking in deep breaths to smell fresh cotton and flowers.

"Hello, Mrs. Goodwin. How are you doing, Mr. Paul?" he said, nodding and smiling at the customers.

While preparing for bed that evening, Dub turned to Mae as she pulled on her cotton nightgown. "Working at the general store, I've learned a great deal about the people here in Morriston. If I'm cleaning the store, I'm low on the scale in their eyes. The coal mining job is the only way to climb higher, give you the lifestyle you want, and put more food on the table. Seeing what Zeke is doing, it's the only way."

"It'll be wonderful to have a few more dresses, fancy things for the children, a bigger home and better kitchen. I can see us now." She looked at the ceiling with a smile, wrapping her arms around herself.

"I can do the work and do it better than anyone."

Over the coming days, instead of going home for lunch, Dub insisted that Mae prepare him a sack lunch to eat, and he went downtown to the Morriston library to research coal mining. Sitting upstairs in the corner of the library behind a tall bookshelf, he read all he could about strip mines, drift mines, slope mines, shaft mines, and all the terminology.

Now he needed the name of the coal mining company and the day and time for the interviews. A good source of information on Upper Orchard came from eavesdropping on the various groups during work breaks. The next day while working at the textile factory, Dub waited by his machine until he saw Lee punch the time clock for a break, then followed behind at a distance.

Lee walked to a group of men squatting under a tall tree with sprawling branches providing ample shade from the intense late morning sun. Smoke swirled upward from their cigarettes through the leaves and glided into the air during the intense conversation. Dub ambled out to the courtyard, sauntering past Lee, then leaned against a factory wall a few feet away, hidden around a corner of the building. He pulled an apple from his pocket, rubbed it on his shirt, and took a bite, staring out into the distance in the opposite direction of the group of men.

"Lee, are you putting in an application for the coal mine?" a man said, tapping the tobacco out of his pipe.

"I don't rightly know yet. I think the colored who operates the machine next to me wants to apply. He's been asking me when the people are coming to town."

"What'd you say?" a couple of the men asked at the same time.

"You think I'd tell him? Of course I didn't tell him they'll be at Smith's Hardware tomorrow. Why should I help him? I don't want a colored taking a job I want, so I'm going there at one p.m. sharp."

Dub tossed his apple in the garbage receptacle and returned to his machine.

After work, he did one final study session at the library, and that night he had Mae prepare his clothes.

"OK, Mae, since the people are coming tomorrow to do the interviews, I wrote out some practice questions. Read these to me," he said, handing her a sheet of paper, "and I'll answer them like you are the man from the mining company."

She chuckled. Sitting in the middle of their bed in her cotton nightgown and hair rolled up in pin curls, she mimicked a man's voice, putting on a serious face. Dub sat on a wooden stool in the corner of the room with his hands on his knees, like a schoolboy. She read the questions intensely. Listening to him answer each question coherently proved to her that he knew about the geography and technicalities of extracting coal as a miner or a loader. He even recited the proper tools to use, at least to the degree one could learn from a book. With each answer, Mae nodded and looked him straight in the eye. After Dub answered the last question, she jumped off the bed, wrapping him in her arms.

"I believe you'll pull this off. I see our future and it's not in this small town." She gave him a passionate kiss. "But we have more to do."

She ran to the kitchen to make sure his clothes were ready. She ironed extra starch into his shirt and pants, brushed off his Sunday hat and shined his shoes, and placed everything neatly in the bedroom armoire for the next day.

On Tuesday morning inside the textile factory, small groups of machinists dotted the machine floor, whispering. Occasionally, a worker craned their neck and chuckled in Dub's direction.

"Do you want something? Should I come over there?" Dub asked after several such incidents of gawking.

The man shook his head and laughed as the group broke up and each man went back to their machine.

When the whistle blew for quitting time, Lee said, "Dub, I may not see you after today, I'm going to work in a high-paying coal job. Sorry you're stuck here."

"You think I'm going to let the likes of you and the rest of your pack make me miss the interviews?" Dub took a step toward Lee.

"Old Benny told us his wife, the librarian, said you wanted all the books you could read about coal mining. No one will hire you. You're just a poor colored that'll never go anywhere or do anything. So I suggest you get down off your high horse and step away from me before I hurt you." Lee furrowed his brow and balled up his fists.

"Or what? What're you going to do? Are you scared I could

do better than you? You're standing here at a simple machine just like me. You aren't any better than me. And I'm not moving."

A figure emerged into Dub's peripheral vision, then he felt a sudden pain that catapulted him toward the cement floor, where his head smacked into the side of his steel machine. He lay prone on the cold surface, rapidly blinking his eyes to focus. Lee and Benny stood over him.

"He never saw it coming, the arrogant bastard," Lee said, spitting tobacco in Dub's direction and walking away to join his friends as they headed toward Smith's Hardware in their work clothes.

Dub slowly rose, noticing small droplets of blood on the machine. He felt his head, and moisture coated his fingers as the cut on his scalp oozed a small amount of blood. He quickly staggered to the doors, clocked out, and ran home.

Mae waited with his starched clothes laid out on the bed and shined shoes on the floor. She'd prepared a hot bowl of water, lye soap, and a washcloth to wash away the grime from the factory.

"What happened to you? You have a bruise on the side of your face and blood in your hair."

"I hate those sons of bitches. I'll tell you about it later. Once they hire me to a coal mining job, we're leaving this godforsaken town."

Mae tended to the cut, and Dub walked briskly out of the house toward Smith's Hardware and arrived in less than fifteen minutes.

CHAPTER 10

THE DARE (1924)

On that Tuesday afternoon, the sun shone bright, and the sky was like a piercing white bedsheet covering the earth. The kind of July heat that turns sweat into glue, pasting clothes to skin. Nevertheless determined, Dub stayed fresh in his best Sunday hat and demanded his body stay cool in a freshly pressed white shirt.

Rounding the corner to the brick-paved street of Smith's Hardware Store, he took in the crowd of people. The long line of men obscured the storefront. At its end, beneath the Smith's Hardware Store sign, hung a broad cloth banner with tall red letters reading, "Tappers Mining Company."

Dub surveyed the three distinct lines of men leading to a long table, each staffed by a military-looking agent in a white button-down shirt and freshly cut hair. One line had only white men. Lee and his friends from the textile plant stood twenty men deep from the front, clothed in the grime from their workday. Sweat from the heat accentuated the patches of dirt. The second line was made up of men speaking mostly Irish and Italian. But he joined the third line of brown-skinned people, the shortest line and the slowest moving, and took his place.

"Yes, brother," the man said, glancing at Dub. "This is the right line. Welcome."

"How long have you been waiting?" Dub asked.

"A few minutes, but by my measure they take five of them to one of us," the man responded, nodding in the direction of the second row. "Let's not even talk about the way they're moving through those folks in the first line. We know what that's about."

The man removed his hat, took out a handkerchief from his pants pocket, and wiped the sweat off his forehead and neck.

Turning to Dub, he said, "Kelvin's the name. I've seen you in church. How'd you hear about this?"

"My name is Dub Brisco. I heard about the mining applications from a guy at work. How about you?"

"My son told me. He works at Smith's. Nobody told him directly. He overheard the store owner talking to the Tappers people early this morning. He ran home on his break and told me to hustle over here. I've been looking for a new job."

"Why?"

"I'm a Pullman porter. It keeps me away from the family too much. I want to move us all out of here but still make decent money and be with them every day. How about you? Why are you here?"

"Pretty much the same reason. A better life. Nothing more for me in Morriston."

Dub peered around Kelvin, glimpsing the line in front. Suddenly, the sun's intensity multiplied to where even his hat offered no reprieve, and the sweat beaded on his face. Appearing to ignore the discomfort, he mumbled the questions and answers that he and Mae reviewed the night before. Dub's eyes sometimes squinted toward the back of Kelvin's head for the answer, rolled up in his eyelids to recall an answer, or stared into the ground as if the answer could spring from the dirt. Failing to remember the answer, he nervously grasped the sheet of paper from inside his pants pocket with practice questions prepared from his studies at the library. Humming songs followed the litany of fidgeting. Dub relaxed, closed his eyes, and breathed rhythmically until Kelvin took a step closer to the table of interviewers.

"What can you tell me about Tappers, Kelvin?" Dub said.

"Not much. The men are from up north in Illinois, somewhere near Kentucky. A rich family owns Tappers. They have a problem with workers going out on strike and can't fill coal orders for the more profitable customers. They want to bring in some men from the South and overseas to replace the strikers, knowing it will piss off the union. The jobs will be filled right away. Working in the railroad, I'll tell you these unions don't mess around when they're striking. The tension between them and management grows, and they start rioting. They can kill people. One time the mining union guys on the train heading up north to West Virginia talked about plans to blow up a building. They aren't having as much success anymore unionizing the mine as they did before the First World War."

"Goodness, Kelvin. Sounds like you learn a lot on that train. But I don't care about pissing off the union, or mine explosions and stuff like that."

"Family and money. Better life. I'm not scared to break a strike either. We take more risks walking around Morriston at night. Right?"

The two men continued talking about their aspirations as the row slowly crept forward. After nearly an hour, the three Tappers men in front of Smith's Hardware Store came into Dub's view. Across the three lines, agents briefly asked questions, then decided whether to give out an application.

Fifteen minutes remained before the two p.m. clock-in time for his second job as janitor at the general store. Dub never arrived late. As the third line edged closer to the Tappers banner, he eyed his watch. Ten minutes before two p.m.

A familiar, anxious voice called his name. He spun around and saw Mae running frantically up the street, looking for him with her apron still tied around her waist. She took in the first line, stopped, and turned to sprint toward the second line, paused, shook her head, and studied the third line, then darted down the row. He waved his hands wildly above his head to attract her attention, but he dared not move an inch out of line for fear of losing his place.

"Mae. What's wrong? Did something bad happen to one of the children?" he asked.

"No. They're fine. The neighbor is with them too. Stay here, stay here. When you didn't stop back home to pick up your apron for the general store, I knew you might be late to work. I told a lie. I'm sorry I lied. I told them you ate some bad food and got sick and would be late. You've never been late, and they want you to come when it all passes through your body, but either way you must clean the store tonight. You'll be docked pay, but they won't sack you. Mr. O'Malley said he'll let you in if the store is locked."

"Thanks. I hope he doesn't find out I'm not sick."

"Good luck." She waved and walked briskly back home.

Dub startled when a voice said, "Next." He looked up to see the recruiter for the third line. The man had slicked-back sandy-red hair, red skin from sitting in the sun without a hat, a toothpick in his mouth, and reading glasses perched on his nose. He beckoned Kelvin with his pointer finger. Kelvin stepped past the white chalk line on the ground at least twelve feet in front of the table that sat under the porch eaves of Smith's Hardware Store.

Dub stepped up to the line and leaned forward, turning his ear toward the recruiter. An isolated word from the recruiter occasionally sprung over the voices of other men in the lines. Kelvin nodded from time to time while the recruiter constantly shook his head as if to say no to anything Kelvin said, and even the recruiter's own statements. The other recruiters paused during their own work to peer over at the sandy-red-haired man and chuckle at the back-and-forth between him and the brown-skinned man.

After a few minutes of dialogue with Kelvin, the words "colored Pullman porters are trying to form a union, but that won't happen at Tappers," clearly resonated from the redhead. Kelvin turned his back to the recruiters, paused, gave a brief expressionless look in Dub's direction, then looked down the street at the train and strode toward the station with a steady gait.

The church bells rang two times, announcing two p.m.

Dub straightened his shirt and stood tall. The sandy-red-haired man hailed Dub in the same manner as Kelvin.

With a smile, Dub said, "Good afternoon, sir, I'm here to interview for a coal miner's job at Tappers."

All three recruiters at the table paused and stared at him.

The recruiter at the far end questioned, "What did he say?"

Sandy-Red repeated, "He said, 'I'm here to interview for a coal miner's job at Tappers.'"

The recruiters laughed. Maintaining the smile, Dub focused his eyes on Sandy-Red, whose eyes peered over the top of his reading glasses straight into Dub's.

The sandy-red-haired man took the glasses off and confirmed, "You said, 'I'm here to interview for a coal miner's job at Tappers?'"

Dub nodded and continued to smile at the sandy-red-haired man.

"You want to be a miner? I think you mean a loader or a mule handler. We got enough of you people doing that unskilled stuff. That's why you don't see a single application form in front of me and I haven't given out one all day. And even if I give you one, can you fill it out? Can you read and write?"

"Yes, sir," Dub replied.

"What makes you qualified for a coal miner job? You ever seen one, boy? Have you ever stepped outside of this town?"

The sun beamed down intensely, turning Dub's neck a dull red. The sweat slowly eased out of his skin, attempting to cool him by draining down his back. He maintained his composure and replied in a monotone voice.

"I operate a big machine in the textile plant. I'm strong and work more than twelve hours a day, sir. I read all the books I could in the library about coal mining. I saw many pictures of coal mines and what you folks do down in the mines. And sir, although I've never left Alabama, I'm willing to go anywhere for a coal miner's job."

"Well, boy, what a speech," Sandy-Red said. "It's been a long day and I haven't let anyone in this line stand in my face as long as you have, especially a fake intellectual. But I'll give you an application and see if Tappers even looks at it, mister smart man. You fill it out and bring it back right here tomorrow morning at seven o'clock. We'll see if there's any job at Tappers suitable for one of you people that can read and write. Maybe they'll let you clean our toilets."

By that time, the only lines with men remaining were the second and third. The first line's recruiter stood in the shade on the porch of Smith's Hardware, smoking cigarettes and observing his sandy-red-haired colleague talk to the few men left like it was a sporting event.

Sandy-Red leaned to his right, reached for the stack of applications handed out to men in the second line, and slowly picked one up. He teasingly waved it in Dub's face. As Dub lifted his hand to retrieve it, the sandy-red man quickly pulled it back. All three Tappers agents laughed. Again, the sandy-red-haired man shook it in Dub's direction. Without blinking, Dub studied the man's eyes, expressionless, reached for the application again, and with controlled strength, managed to pull it from Sandy-Red's strong grip.

"Thank you, sir," Dub said. He nodded, turned around with a straight back, and walked away calmly. The few men left in the lines quietly and sympathetically tracked his steps.

Sandy-Red said, "Next. At least the dirty Scots have worked the mines over there. The dirt under their nails proves it. I don't think the savages have coal, or mines for that matter, in Africa, and then they want to come here and talk all superior-like."

Dub continued walking with the same posture to work at the general store, a couple of short blocks around the corner.

"Well, hello, Dub. Are you better?" O'Malley, the boss, said.

Dub said, "Sorry I'm late."

"Dub, you look like you came from a funeral in that starched white shirt and hat. Where's your apron? You sure you're ready to work here, or are you dressed for a job interview?"

Dub's mouth opened, yet nothing came out.

"It's OK, Dub. Make sure everything is done before you go. I want my store spotless before I open in the morning. No cutting corners. And be sure to give me enough notice if Tappers hires you."

O'Malley paid Dub for working only half a day, even though Dub worked eight hours cleaning and restocking shelves. Dub did not complain about the pay.

Arriving home from the general store after ten o'clock that evening, Dub sat down and filled out the Tappers paperwork. He took his time and used his best handwriting, answering each question. When finished, he bathed quickly and had a restless night of sleep, occasionally waking up to check the time and glance at the application sitting near the factory uniform that Mae had washed and pressed. Dub usually left the house at five o'clock in the morning to clock in by five-thirty. By leaving home a bit earlier, he would deliver the form to the Tappers agents well before seven a.m., although the agent had instructed him to bring it "at seven."

It took Dub ten minutes to walk over to Smith's Hardware

Store, where Tappers had interviewed the day before. The agents busied themselves taking the sign down and folding the worktable.

Dub walked up to the sandy-red-haired man and said, "I have my application filled out, sir," holding it out for him.

Sandy-Red said, "Sorry, boy. You're late. We don't take these after five a.m. Don't you clock in at five-thirty like the other men? You people are mighty lazy and dumb. You're the only colored we gave an application to, and you couldn't turn it in on time. That's why you people don't move up in life. You can't follow simple instructions."

"With all due respect, sir, it's exactly five o'clock now, but I heard you say bring it at seven o'clock, but I apologize if this is late. Please accept it. I misunderstood the time."

"My, my, my, boy, you're so articulate. You look clean. Fellas, check out this boy. You think he could be a coal miner with his clean looks? I prefer them Scots with dirty nails."

The other agents chuckled and finished packing.

"Boy, just because somebody taught you how to talk, read, and write, I'll take your application and decide if we have a job for a good strong colored to read instructions on bottles of soap to clean Tappers's bathrooms and offices."

"Again, sir, I'm applying to work underground."

"You'll be lucky if we hire you at all. Why do we need you? Did you see those foreigners? They can run rings around the likes of you, and they're more reliable. I might as well take your application. I'm paid by the head that I bring to them anyway." The sandy-red-haired man yanked the paper out of Dub's hand and turned around.

After dropping off the document, Dub jogged down the block and turned the corner. Looking in the direction of the textile plant, he paused. He turned around and took two steps toward where the Tappers agents continued to pack. He stopped and shook his head and stared at the side of the red brick building with large blue cursive letters, "Grain and Feed." His fist slammed into the dried clay over and over, ignoring the men that slowed down and shook their heads in his direction as his skin started to shred and blood rose to the surface.

Dub finally turned away from the wall, feeling a muscular hand touch his shoulder. Kelvin, the Pullman porter he'd met in line the previous day, guided him back to the sidewalk and escorted him through town in the same direction as dozens of other men in tan work pants, heavy black leather boots, and other uniforms.

When the two men approached the train station, Kelvin patted Dub on the back and headed toward the Gulf, Mobile & Northern train, with its four coaches and caboose, that stood quietly on the tracks, spewing white smoke from below while waiting for attention from its engineer and other caretakers. Dub and others continued as they did habitually every workday, walking toward the outskirts of town, and filed into the textile factory.

That same morning, at home, Mae dropped to her knees the minute Dub left the house with the application and prayed out loud for a full five minutes. "God, I pray that you see fit to give that job to my husband and send my family north. I want more for me and my kids."

CHAPTER 11

COMINGS AND GOINGS (1924)

Days after delivering their seventh child, Chloe, Mae fully embraced the prospect of leaving their crowded two-bedroom home for a new life up north in Abingdon, Illinois, and eagerly awaited any news. She scrutinized the post each day for anything from Tappers Mining Company.

Midmornings, Mae promptly walked down the front sidewalk of the house to the mailbox when the crackling sound of heavy postman boots crushed gravel from the street. The routine commenced three houses down. Ten steps of crackling gravel, then pause for ten seconds while the mail went into a box. The second set of ten steps of crackling gravel, then pause for ten seconds. Mae met the postman within five seconds of his third set of ten steps, sporting flour and bread dough stuck to her hands and a stained white apron.

Wednesday in the third week after Dub applied for the job, Mae ran to the mailbox as usual. The postman, wearing gray flannel pants and a gray summer-cotton shirt with a black tie pulled snugly under his neck, removed several letters from his sack, inspecting the front and back of each. Shuffling through the stack of mail in his hand, the postman paused to more closely inspect an unusual thick brown envelope. His thumb reached beneath the glue sealed flap.

"Good morning, sir," Mae said, running off the porch.

The postman struggled to stuff the brown envelope back in his mailbag.

"Wait," Mae said, her hand and arm extended only a few feet from the postman's chest.

Reluctantly, he quickly handed her all the Brisco correspondence, including the unique brown envelope, and turned his head without acknowledging her.

Mae brushed hair from her face with the back of her hand while holding the mail in her other hand, then said, "Thank you, sir," with a smile and a nod.

He walked away to the next mailbox.

Mae walked slowly back into the house, staring at the envelope, breathing deeply like she had run five miles instead of several feet. Once inside, she leaned the brown envelope against the salt and pepper shakers in the middle of the kitchen table, stepping back to inspect the delicate object.

"I can't wait for Dub to come home for lunch. But until then I'll just keep myself busy."

The anticipation kept her moving around the room, rotating between kneading the bread dough, putting it in the pan, basting the mound with butter, and ironing the bag of linen from the hotel. Each time she switched tasks, her eyes gravitated, over and over, to a symbol of her future.

Tappers Mining Company
Mr. Robert Ray Williamson, Personnel Office
803 Winston Street
Abingdon, Illinois

Even while making Dub's lunch two hours later, Mae made sure the letter stayed in its place. Absorbed in the anticipation of his arrival and envisioning his reaction, she did not hear him walk up behind her and wrap his arms around her small, aproned waist.

He placed a warm kiss on her neck and said, "Mm-mm, freshly baked bread. I'm ready to eat."

Mae jumped with a brief startled sound. Although Dub continued complimenting the tempting smells in the kitchen, Mae quickly ran, with him hanging on to her body, to the table where the letter resided in its spot. He did not see it sitting on the table, but once he focused in that direction, his eyes expanded and all movement froze. Bouncing up and down with excitement, Mae grabbed the envelope and shoved it in his hands with the address facing up. His hands shook when he saw the name Tappers rendered prominently on the front.

"Open it. Open it," Mae said, shaking his arm.

To preserve the envelope, he opened the letter slowly and gently, slipping his pinky finger under the partially opened flap, gliding it across the seal. He removed three stiff pages. As they'd stood in line for the Tappers interviews, Kelvin had told Dub that these types of letters started with the word "Congratulations" if you were hired, and "Unfortunately" if you were rejected. This communication started with neither. It began with *We received your application.*

He slowly and silently studied the words, then, reciting a few, he said, "The agent interviewing you at the application intake said that you are a Negro who can read and speak well and looks clean and presentable. We are looking for a trustworthy Negro to clean the executive offices and supervise four other janitors."

He raised his eyes from the page with a blank expression.

"Janitor? How's that a step up? That's a step back and less pay," Mae said.

"No, this isn't the job I wanted. But I guess it's something.

They clearly want me, so this could be an opportunity for something."

He continued reading the job description.

He said, "They are saying, 'To start, we will pay you thirty cents per hour.'" He paused. "But that's OK with me. I make fifteen cents on the factory line and another five cents at the store." Looking out the window again, he said, "Moving north we elevate from the confines of Morriston and working two jobs. Nothing more exists for us down here. Oh, I guess I should finish the letter, huh? They go on to say, 'We offer twenty-five dollars to help with moving, but this will not be given to you until you arrive at the job site. The last page of this letter is a list of homes with rooms for Negroes where you can stay until your family joins you. You can also find a home where the Negroes live in the Tarboro area in Abingdon, Illinois.'"

Mae waited with anticipation while Dub finished the rest in silence, his face expressionless. He finally looked up.

"Mae, we're moving to Abingdon, Illinois."

Husband and wife needed no discussion. As they had done before the interview, they embraced in a serene stillness, then smiled at each other.

"With the extra money and you being a supervisor and taking care of all the executives, we are going to have so much more, and some status," Mae said as she spun around the kitchen. "What do you need from me, my prosperous husband?"

"Only you and these kids by my side. We start fresh, leaving all the pain behind. We'll talk more tonight after work."

Mae set his lunch on the table while Dub washed his hands in the closet to prepare for his second job. Neither one said much more. Mae hummed joyful songs around the kitchen, watching Dub eat his food pensively.

After Dub's departure to the general store, in the quiet house with children napping, Mae washed and stored the lunch dishes. A bag of clean linen from the hotel awaited ironing in the corner, yet she briefly ignored its presence. The view of the richness of life lured her to the front of the house.

A survey of the room revealed how far the couple had progressed from the sparse bedroom they had occupied at her aunt and uncle's home. When Miss Clara had passed earlier in the year, Mae had received all of Clara's living room and dining room furniture, antique place settings, silver flatware, and crystal stemware. The sturdy china cabinet from Clara drew Mae's hand, and she felt the warmth of the polished wood. Inside sat a stack of porcelain hand-painted teacups belonging to Clara's mother. Mae moved to the window and stroked Clara's lace curtains that neighbors admired from the street.

A white panel delivery truck rolled up in front of the mailbox. The man alighted from the seat, waved at Mae, and tipped his newsboy cap. Adjusting thin suspenders holding up oversized work pants, he walked around the truck to unload a large white linen bag from the cargo bed. Mae opened the front door as the man hoisted the load over his shoulder. She placed a finger over her lips. The man nodded and walked quietly to the kitchen, delivering the items for pressing from the hotel. When he saw the other bag in the corner, he raised his eyebrows and two fingers. Mae shrugged and nodded. He mimicked a laugh and Mae smiled. Waving goodbye, he turned and tiptoed to the door. As Mae shut the door behind him, Genese and Calvin cried in unison.

On his way to the job at the general store, Dub stopped at the post office and sent a telegram accepting the position at Tappers in the manner described in the letter and committing to start exactly one month from that day. Throughout the several hours of work, Dub stopped to write items on a list of things he and Mae needed to do in preparation for the move. *Sell or rent the house. Sell furniture. School for children. Save money to buy train tickets for family. Find out how to ride a train. Find house to rent. Go see Mama and Tim. Resign jobs.* In between adding tasks to the list, the note stayed tucked inside his shirt pocket. Upon his return home that night, he sat down with Mae.

"Let's outline what we need to accomplish over the coming weeks to make this move," Dub said, pulling out his list. "There's a lot to do, including preparing the kids. We need to sell this house or rent it to a relative or something. I don't think we can take all this stuff with us either, so let's dispose of as much as we can. Tappers said we can find housing in Abingdon. As soon as we arrive, we must ask if they have schools for young colored children. Oh my, a lot to do in a little bit of time. This is happening so fast."

He closed his eyes, letting out a deep breath.

Mae touched his hand. "We'll get it all done. I'll attend to the house and start selling stuff. The pastor can help too and announce to the congregation what we need. Some people in the neighborhood will help spread the word and find somebody to buy this house."

"Mae, I can't believe this is really happening. This has to work out."

"When will you tell Betsey? She'll find out anyway through the church. I don't want her over here in a tirade because some busybodies spread it through the grapevine. And what about Tim?"

"I heard from Mama that Tim is going off to some college called Talladega, so why do I need to think about him? I'll tell her sometime this week about our plans. I just need to move on. I'm following what my daddy did."

"Just remember, when you talk with Betsey, all your money is for us and our kids. And don't tell her about the twenty-five dollars Tappers is giving you and the extra wages."

It took Tappers twenty-four hours to send a telegram to confirm receipt of his wire and welcome him as a new employee with the title janitorial supervisor at thirty cents per hour, giving specifics on when and how to report. Once Dub received a reply, he resigned his job at O'Malley's General Store to have that time to help Mae sell the house and the belongings that they could not take on the train.

He worked at the textile factory another three weeks to make money for the family's rail tickets, while Mae searched through the church and friends to find a furnished house to rent in the Tarboro community of Abingdon. At the end of the three weeks, the house sold, and Dub quit his factory job. He had not spoken to Lee since the day of their altercation.

"Lee, you won't see me tomorrow. Tappers hired me. I'm leaving this place."

"They picked you? For what? To clean toilets?"

"As a matter of fact, Lee, I'll be a janitorial supervisor, the boss of four other people, and making more money too."

"I knew they wouldn't let you be a coal miner. You got shot down. So you're moving to supervise the toilet cleaners? How stupid. Good luck to you, Mr. Janitor, sir." After retrieving his punch card from the time-clock machine, Lee turned to Dub. "Don't expect much."

"Well, Lee, it seems they didn't hire you for any job. Remember, you planted the idea when you told me about the interviews. My life has no barriers, and my determination has no boundaries. So thanks for the information about Tappers."

***

Neither Dub nor Mae had yet experienced traveling by train. Dub remembered Kelvin was a Pullman porter, and he tracked him down through a friend at the post office. Learning the address, he got a pleasant surprise.

"Wow, Kelvin. In my walks through the neighborhood, I always wondered who lived in this house. I spotted a woman and children in the yard. Believe it or not, my wife and I resided here for a couple of years with the previous owner, Miss Clara, after first marrying. I'm awfully glad to find you home."

"I'm usually not in town. As I told you, being a porter keeps me away more than my wife and I like. Any news about your application to Tappers?"

"Yes, but instead of a coal miner position, I got a janitorial supervisor's job cleaning the administration buildings. But at least it's offering me more than I make now. I accepted the job and will head up to Illinois in a matter of days. My plan is to gain the favor of all the executives that I meet, and to convince them to move me into the coal mines within a year. How about you?"

"They're afraid of me. The Negro Pullman porters have been talking about forming a union. Those agents questioned my union support if I came to Tappers. So they didn't give me an application. That's OK. I'm making great money, and that is why I could afford this house. Instead of changing jobs, it may be better to stay with the railroad but move up north to a big city. My kids are at the age where they need exposure to more opportunities. Anyway, what can I do for you?"

"I've never been on a train. My wife hasn't either. I need to learn what to do so I don't run into problems. Like everything else, Negroes can and cannot do certain things riding the rails. Right? I thought you could help me out."

"Glad to." Kelvin explained the protocols of riding the railroad, from how to buy tickets to where to wait in the stations and where to sit in the car. Kelvin also relayed a little information about Abingdon, Illinois, from traveling through that station.

"Where do you plan to live in Abingdon?" Kelvin said.

"Through our church, we were put in touch with some people that got us a house to rent in the Tarboro area," Dub said. "That's where Tappers told us to live too. I guess that is where the Negroes reside, right?"

"Here's what I know. Any home you rent in Tarboro is owned by someone in the Tappers family. Way back when Tappers started that coal mine, they bought all the property and built houses for their employees. They controlled almost the whole town, including the stores and other services. Every employee rented their home from Tappers and bought food and other needs from Tappers. But the company doesn't own the homes anymore. They were either sold to the people living in them, if they could afford it, or sold to someone in the Tappers family. Now, that person in the family rents them out. My understanding from asking around is that the family is not too bad to deal with."

The hardest task on Dub's list was talking to Tim and Betsey. Although only several blocks separated his home from Betsey's, the families rarely saw each other. And when they did, it was either in the opening or closing greeting of the Sunday church service. Other than church, Dub and Mae did not pass Betsey's block or other places she frequented. Mae, who purchased the food needed for the family, did not frequent the grocery store during Tim's work hours.

On one of their final mornings in Morriston, Dub left the house early to catch both Tim and Betsey at home. Large clouds played with the sun, first covering it up, then letting it shine. He paid no attention to the weather. Walking slowly, he practiced telling Betsey and Tim no to requests for money. With six children, Dub did not dare give a penny to Betsey without incurring the wrath of Mae.

Along the walk, he waved to people he had not seen since moving from Betsey's home nine years ago or since Junie's funeral two years prior. Others approached to chat and catch up on their family's health. The closer he got to Betsey's house, the more the appearance of the neighborhood changed. The homes became smaller and less well maintained due to the lower financial capabilities of the residents.

Nearing the destination, Dub saw lights shining through Tim's bedroom window. His pace slowed. He hesitantly climbed the front stoop, turned the doorknob, and pushed the door open. Peeking his head inside, the silence caused him pause. Then he proceeded inside toward the hallway and peered inside the first bedroom. Betsey's space looked tidy with a clean, freshly made bed. He turned to lightly knock on Tim's door.

Tim abruptly opened it.

"What?" Tim paused. "Oh, Dub. What are you doing here? Something happen to Mae or the kids?"

"No, we're all fine. Where's Mama?"

"Right behind you," Betsey said.

"Oh, the house was so quiet."

"I went into the outhouse. Why are you here? I hope you brought something for my jar for the first time in almost ten years."

"Well, Mama, let's go to the kitchen."

Dub looked around as the three walked into the kitchen. He briefly smiled upon seeing the only picture of Tuttle and the cabin in Green Creek; it was one of the few times his father had embraced him. Betsey and the other children stood in front.

The clean kitchen received a pleasant smile like the rest of the home, although the satisfaction faded once he spotted a few water stains on the ceiling. Pursed lips choked back a complaint to Betsey on the lack of roof maintenance.

"I have some breakfast ready if you're hungry. Want some?" Betsey strode over to the cabinet reaching for a plate.

"No, thanks. Mae took care of me."

"Of course," Betsey said, rolling her eyes and retreating to the kitchen table.

He held out the chair for Betsey to sit at the table. Tim proceeded to the cabinet, grabbed a plate, and added three pieces of bacon from the skillet, spooned on some scrambled eggs, and added a slice of cornbread from a baking pan.

Dub waited patiently while Tim settled his breakfast on the table. Betsey sat with folded hands. She straightened the collar on her freshly cleaned and starched dress, then smoothed back recently washed hair.

"Mama, you look good."

Betsey smiled.

"I'll get to the point. Next week, the family and I are moving north to Abingdon, Illinois. I got a job at a coal mine. Now, I won't be in the mine, but I'll be a janitorial supervisor with several men working under me. With my big family, I need to make more money, and this is a good opportunity. Everything is arranged and in order. We already sold the house."

Betsey said, "I heard at church. I should have been the first you told. I wanted to see how long it took you to make your way here to tell your mama. You're such an ungrateful son. You never give me money and you never visit. That bitchy wife of yours keeps you away. Just because she's Creole doesn't make her any better than the rest of us."

"Mama, please don't start. Especially talking about my wife." Dub stood abruptly to leave. "Why did I bother to come here. I guess I should be happy you're sober."

"Just make sure you leave something in the jar before you go. Maybe not. You're too afraid of your wife."

Dub turned and stormed out of the house.

Tim threw the fork onto his plate and ran after Dub.

"Hey, Dub." Tim stopped him on the porch.

"What? Look, Tim, I don't have time to deal with Mama. This is why I don't come here. You deal with her."

"It's not about her. I need your help or at least your advice. There is this girl. Her name is Kate. I love her."

"OK. So marry her. You're old enough. What do you want from me?"

"She's having our baby. Her parents are sending her away."

"Aren't you going to college? Sorry. I can't help. I don't have time to help you deal with this. I have my own children to worry about. Go talk to Betsey. Tim, sometimes you just got to walk away from people who drain you. Daddy did it. Our other siblings, including Zeke, did it too. It's my turn."

More clouds gathered in the sky and small drops of rain began to fall. Dub walked home at the same pace he'd arrived. While the rain's intensity increased, Dub raised his face to the sky, welcoming the baptism.

After another week of planning and packing, the entire Dub Brisco clan of eight took the train north to Abingdon, Illinois, with only clothes, minimal other necessities, and food to ration for several days. They dressed in their Sunday best, boarding stark accommodations near the locomotive. The cars farther away from the locomotive had dining and other comforts, including a special place to store the luggage. However, Dub knew from Kelvin that the family was not welcome in those areas.

Dub guided his crew into the appropriate car, found seats, and stacked their possessions neatly around their legs like a protective fortress. The children considered the train ride an adventure, while the parents focused on making sure they followed Kelvin's advice to avoid any problems and avoid breaking any laws.

After two days in transit, Dub and family arrived in Abingdon, Illinois.

CHAPTER 12

MOVING ON (1924)

Dub's life in Abingdon started the way he and Mae had anticipated.

"Look at it," Mae said, laying eyes on their furnished rental home in the Tarboro community. "It's not as grand as Miss Clara's house, but I'm willing to bet it's better than what Zeke and Zelda have in West Virginia. Can we put a swing on the porch? I can picture myself rocking our babies every night. See how the two walnut trees give the right amount of shade with the white snowball bushes along the front porch? Everyone will know this is our house once I'm done with it."

After moving in, Dub built the swing as the first improvement to the property. He hung it from two long, thick chains and painted it white like a southern swing, just as Mae wanted. To make it strong and impervious to rot, he used cedar wood so Mae could sit all the children around her for years to come.

At breakfast the next morning, he said, "Mae, I have no pretenses that life will be easy here. The way the Tappers agents acted during the interviews down in Morriston makes it clear that Tappers is no different than the South. But I'll keep my head down. My job now is to lead a team of janitors in cleaning the offices, cafeterias, doctor's office, and locker rooms. I'll do my job one hundred twenty-five percent." He nodded and took a last bite of bacon.

"I understand. I'm happy we have this beautiful home, and with your ambition, one day we'll have something as lovely as when we stayed with Miss Clara. I hate that we had to sell off the things she gave us. But at least we kept some of the fine china pieces."

After establishing the family in Abingdon, the couple retained some resemblances of their life in the South and kept the same vision. Each day fulfilled Mae's dream of prosperity. Her world became the four walls of the house, decorated with floral and lace curtains at every window.

The kitchen represented the heart of the house. Larger than the kitchen in Morriston, the new house fit a table for their family of eight. It not only served for family meals but also as a place of learning for the children. Mae transformed the kitchen from dining to classroom several times throughout the day. Like a chameleon, the table became a baker's table, chef's table, or butcher's table as the need arose. White metal cabinets holding the dishes, food, and sundries lined the wall above a buffet and sink. From sunup to sundown, Mae had something cooking on her six-burner stove or baking in the oven.

She did the laundry on a small screened-in porch behind the kitchen. It barely fit the two washtubs, one tub for washing and the other for rinsing, each topped by a wringer with rollers to squeeze out the water. The porch barely had enough room in the corner for the mandatory iron and starch at the ready to perfect the outward appearance of each family member. Dub built shelves to one side as a pantry for storing the jars of vegetables and fruit Mae canned from their garden.

What helped elevate her above the neighbors was the fact that this home was newer and one of the few with electricity and indoor plumbing. The bungalow held three bedrooms for the family to spread out.

Mae had a system that commenced at four o'clock in the morning and ended at nine o'clock at night. Dub woke up before the sun to find washed-and-starched clothes. He proudly put on his newsboy-style hat, gave his wife a kiss, and retrieved the black metal lunch pail and coffee thermos she'd bought as a gift for the new job. In her best handwriting, she'd painted Dub's name in red letters on the side of the pail. He commenced the two-mile walk to work, whistling and smelling the air.

On his first day at Tappers, he made sure to arrive well in advance of starting time. The walk to work began around five o'clock in the morning, a journey he'd practiced the previous day. Following a procession of other brown-skinned men from Tarboro for the two miles, Dub finally saw a wooden sign spanning a dirt road that said "TAPPERS MINING COMPANY" in bold red letters, held up by two wooden posts on either side. He did not suppress the grin on his face as he entered the gates with other brown and white men all mingled together.

In the late nineteenth century, the first Mr. Jackson Tappers bought a swath of land, speculating coal underground. Over time, he recruited other miners and gradually built a coal camp that grew into an entire community with a church, housing, a general store, a school, a doctor's office, a blacksmith and stable for the horses that pulled the coal carts from the mines, and a bar for the men's recreation.

Although the residents worked together, Jack Tappers ensured his camp kept people separate when it came to their personal lives. As the Tapperses sold off property, Abingdon evolved, yet the location of the rail lines assured a separation of people remained in place. Tarboro came to define the outer edge of Abingdon and its community to the south of the railroad.

"Scab! Go back to the South! You came here to steal a job?" said a man, arms waving.

Dub pivoted to return home, but thought, *OK, Dub. Kelvin told you these unions don't mess around when they're striking. They viciously protect their jobs. But if Kelvin can dare break a strike line, I can too.*

He took a deep breath and continued the journey into the mining facility. Glancing at the instructions on the letter retrieved from his pocket, he scanned for signs directing him to the personnel office.

A stealth presence followed the moment he passed through the gate. Perched on a horse, a long-legged, broad-shouldered man with thick curly hair straining to escape from under a wide-brimmed hat, slowly and quietly trailed Dub from twelve feet behind, noting each step he took down the campus streets. Again, he pulled the letter from his pocket to inspect the instructions. A deep voice made him freeze midstep.

"What do you have there?" the man said.

His shirt bore a badge displaying the words "Tappers Security."

He said, "What's that paper you got?"

Dub handed the man the single sheet of paper from Tappers with his hiring information.

"I said, give me the papers," the man said.

"Sir, that's all I have."

"I know a union supporter when I see one, boy. Turn around and open your coat. I want all of them papers you're about to hand out."

Dub unbuttoned his coat and spread it out like wings.

While Dub slowly turned around, the man said, "The one thing Mr. Tappers won't tolerate is striking and the United Mine Workers union. I learned how they're using you coloreds now to do their work. You walk in here dressed all nice. That won't work with me."

Dub stopped, stared, and stood silently glaring at the man who inspected him up and down with narrowed eyes.

The man proceeded to read the letter. "Oh, you're the colored man hired from down south to replace the head janitor," he said, handing back the letter. "They tell me all the new folks coming each day. But why are you coming dressed like you're in charge of something and a lunch pail with your name on it all fancy-like? You're just a nothing janitor hired to clean our shit. You best be careful and know your place. I'm watching."

As quietly as the man had approached, he rode off, sitting up tall on the horse.

Beyond the Tappers entrance sign rose several stacks billowing black and white smoke. Small bits of coal dust landed on Dub's skin, welcoming him. Turning left as the sign indicated toward the personnel office, he saw a conveyor nestled on top of a wooden trellis bridge, carrying coal from an imposing building up a hill to a smaller building at the base of a chimney. To find the personnel office, he crossed a railroad track where a line of empty steel rail cars disappeared into the largest building on the campus. He recognized the company names displayed on each car from seeing them pass by his house. On the opposite side of the building, the cars exited full of coal.

Slowing his walk and gazing at the massive view, Dub saw another sign pointing to the "Coke Oven & Yard." Looking in the direction the arrow pointed, he marveled at the expansiveness of the Tappers campus compared to the textile factory in Morriston.

He apprehensively approached the personnel office, which bore a sign in the window reading "Closed." While waiting for it to open, he took in the activity up and down the roads of the campus. Some people wore uniforms, and others wore casual street clothes or suits. A woman finally walked up, holding out a key to unlock the door. She paused and stepped back briefly with wide eyes upon seeing Dub standing next to the stairs, watching her. He quickly backed away several feet, whereupon she stepped forward to unlock the door.

"Pardon me, ma'am," Dub said with a slight nod, removing his hat. She did not look at him and unlocked the door. After opening the door, she spoke to other arriving workers while Dub followed her inside.

He slowly walked up the two steps into the wood-frame building, which revealed a room full of desks with name plates on each one. The woman walked to the first desk, which held a name plate reading, "Jean Crenshaw, Intake Secretary," and sat in the wooden chair behind it.

"I'm reporting for work, ma'am. My name is Dublin Brisco," he said, bowing slightly from the waist and removing his hat again.

"Stay right there," Miss Crenshaw said. She stood, picked up her purse, and walked into a back room.

I guess Zeke's saying Negroes and white people socializing at the mines doesn't apply to Tappers, Dub thought, stepping back beyond an arm's length from the desk, then patiently waiting without moving an inch.

While he stood in front of Miss Crenshaw's desk, more people arrived and took their places behind the other desks. As they did, Dub scoped out their names and titles. A boyish-looking man dressed in a fine white shirt, black wool pants, and silk tie strode into the room and sat erect at a desk at the far end of the office behind a "James Tappers" name plate. Each person smiled at the young man. He casually nodded in return.

Finally, Miss Crenshaw returned with her purse, sat behind the desk, and crossed her legs, balancing a pair of glasses on her nose to read.

"Now, let me find your name on the intake sheet," she said, pulling a piece of paper out of a desk drawer and slowly running her finger down the list of names.

"I'm sure my name is there . . . I hope?" Dub said, again pulling the letter from Tappers from his pocket and unfolding it with shaking hands.

Dampness oozed from his armpits and palms. He leaned over the desk holding the document out toward Miss Crenshaw, while also peeking at the list of names, trying to find his, reading upside down.

Ignoring Dub, Miss Crenshaw got to the bottom of the page, then rescanned the names a second time using a ruler.

"Is this letter a mistake?" Dub asked. "It is from Mr. Robert Ray Williamson here at Tappers. I don't see my name either."

"Ah. There you are," Ms. Crenshaw said. "Prisco, Dublin."

"No, ma'am, my last name is Brisco, *B* not *P*. That is a mistake. That's why I didn't see it either. What a relief."

"Oh. Are you sure, Dublin? We don't make those kinds of mistakes. Let me see what we sent to you."

He extended the letter again. Miss Crenshaw adjusted the glasses on her nose to read and study the words.

"I see," she said. "You are correct, your name is spelled with a *B*. Perfect. Now we have confirmed it. Janitorial supervisor. Wow. That's a big job for someone like you. But I guess someone thought you could handle it. Let me find the paperwork for you to fill out and put you to work. You can write? Oh, of course you can, otherwise you wouldn't have this job. Right?"

Miss Crenshaw spun around in her chair, pulled a file with Dub's name out of a drawer behind her, then walked stiffly down the row to the man sitting behind the desk with the "James Tappers" nameplate.

Following her movements became his visual tour of the office. One that Dub and his team would clean. With slight movements of his chin, he counted fourteen desks. As he stood waiting, each desk and chair were occupied as the workers filed in. *Some of those tops and sides need shining,* he thought. *The pine floor looks waxed, but I can see a few dull spots. I'll tell the guys to hit those better. Cobwebs in the ceiling-fan blades, and the wastebaskets have food and drink stains on the outside. Look at the sagging file cabinet handles, and paint chips on a few of the walls with water stains. Lots of work to do. I can do a lot here and make a great impression.*

Miss Crenshaw reached her destination, briefly spoke to James Tappers, and handed him Dub's file. He looked up quizzically at Dub, then followed Miss Crenshaw down the row to her workstation.

"You can call me Dub," he said, extending his hand as the young man approached Ms. Crenshaw's desk. "Are you *the* Mr. Tappers?"

"I'm part of the Tappers family. Jimmy's the name," he said hesitantly, then lightly grasped Dub's hand. "So you are the new janitorial supervisor. My grandfather asked me to orient all new employees this week. I will show you the campus and all the buildings your team will clean according to the job description in your file here. Your team is pretty much cleaning every administrative building. Miss Crenshaw here doesn't take well to chitchat, so we should move along."

Jimmy spent the morning escorting Dub through the sections of the campus where the mine workers extracted coal and explaining the scope of the cleaning job. The factory whistle blared, signaling the lunch break, just as the tour took Jimmy and Dub toward the cafeteria.

"This is the Tappers cafeteria. Some people bring their lunch from home, and some buy their lunch," Jimmy said. "This is where janitors sit," he said, pointing to a side of the cafeteria that reminded Dub of the third line with only brown people in which he'd stood to apply for the job.

Designed like a military mess hall, the cafeteria consisted of one long rectangular wooden building with double doors at each end marked "Entrance" and "Exit." Windows lined the sides, revealing the ebb and flow of activity throughout the Tappers campus and serving to remind those eating to change shifts or return to work.

To the right of the entrance, cooks and servers handed plated meals or a simple bag with a sandwich across a kitchen counter. Whether the employee received a sandwich bag or a plate varied based upon the worker's uniform. Workers learned quickly which line to enter to receive their food if they chose to pay a portion of their wages to eat from the kitchen.

Three rows of wooden picnic tables with seating for eight people each sat between the Entrance and Exit signs. Workers sitting in each row and table were grouped according to their status in the company. Otherwise, no signs or guidance existed as to how to navigate the cafeteria.

"Follow me," Jimmy said, walking up to the kitchen counter. "Rita, this is Dub, the new janitorial supervisor, and it's his first day. He has a lunchbox, but still fix him a lunch, free for today. I showed him where the janitors usually sit. Dub, I'm joining my brother over on the other side of the room. I'll come back and get you after I finish my lunch and we'll tour the executive office, doctor's office, and locker rooms and then go back to Miss Crenshaw to process some paperwork. Rita, I'll let you take over from here."

"Sure thing, Mr. Tappers. I'll have Clayton bring your plate right away too."

"Thanks, Rita. I'll take my leave now."

Rita nodded and instinctively leaned toward the kitchen pass-through window and yelled, "Clayton. Get Mr. Jimmy his food."

"So, Dub, what's your last name?" Rita asked as she inspected him up and down, her hands resting on shapely hips enhanced by an apron tied tightly around her waist.

"I'm Dublin Brisco, ma'am."

"Well, Dublin Brisco, you talk mighty proper; tell me about

yourself while I fix your lunch. I'm sure it's better than what's in that fancy lunchbox."

As she prepared Dub a ham sandwich on white bread with coleslaw and a glass of ice water, he told her the circumstances behind his arrival and about his family. At the same time, he glanced at the cooks preparing plates of baked chicken, mashed potatoes, and green beans, with tall glasses of sweet tea. The men in suits, including Jimmy, casually received the healthy portions of food, ignorant of the longing looks from workers receiving ham sandwiches, or workers carrying lunch pails or bags with homemade food.

"Well, well. I believe you're my new neighbor in Tarboro. Are you the new family that recently moved in next to the railroad tracks? I saw a bunch of kids too," Rita said.

She spoke quickly, rarely taking a breath, as it appeared her brain worked so fast her mouth had to keep moving to capture all she wanted to say. Dub struggled to respond and engage in any amount of conversation or even ask Rita questions to learn more about Tappers and the environment.

"Yes," Dub said.

Rita scrunched her face. "Well, my, my. I heard from some Tarboro neighbors y'all are a little snooty, but really, you're OK."

"That's what you heard? Hmm. Miss Rita—"

"Ahh, let's just move on. Dublin, glad to meet you and to hear your story."

"Just call me Dub. So, janitors sit over here?"

"Well, yes, at any of these three tables. But this table is where your janitors are sitting now and where they usually sit. Come on, I'll introduce you."

She set his bag with the ham sandwich, the cup of coleslaw, and his glass of water in front of an empty space on the bench where four men sat dressed in brown uniforms. Each one had either a lunch pail or nominal food in front of them. When they saw Rita walk up with Dub following, the conversation paused.

"Fellas, let me introduce you to the new janitorial supervisor, Dub Brisco," Rita said. "Jimmy Tappers brought him in here for his first day and Mr. Jimmy will be back to finish his tour around the campus here. You men tell him about the work and introduce yourselves. I've got to get back to the kitchen. By the by, his is the new family that moved into old man Greisen Tapperss's rental house . . . the one with all the kids. Nice meeting you, Dub. I look after us Negroes here as much as I can. Let me know what I can do to help. Tell these guys about yourself."

And off Rita went, talking to herself but loud enough for everyone in sight to hear. "Why is the pitcher of tea empty over there?" she asked as she disappeared into the kitchen. "Oh my goodness, and here comes the old man. Where is Clayton? Good gracious, that pitcher should have been over at the Tapperses' table. Clayton . . ."

Expecting one of the men to speak first, Dub sat down and nodded at the four men one at a time. Receiving nothing but silence, he reached out his hand to the man on his right and asked his name.

"Jeremiah Clemmons," he said shaking Dub's hand, and introduced the other three. Over the next thirty minutes, Dub conducted a question-and-answer session, but none of the men volunteered much information or asked many questions.

"Let's go, Dub," Jimmy said when he returned. "The next place I want to take you is the executive office, the location from where my family runs things around here. My grandfather is particular about what he wants done with the cleaning and maintenance. And this is when I tell you about my family history."

Dub waved goodbye to the janitors. "Pleasure meeting each of you. I'll talk with you after I visit the campus."

The men nodded and quickly returned to eating.

Dub said, "Mr. Jimmy, this is the part of the tour I've been truly waiting for. I want to make sure I do right by your family."

Jimmy Tappers had graduated from college just a few months before taking on the new responsibilities of his legacy. As the grandson of Jack Tappers, he had to learn the business from the ground up with the expectation he would take over one day. As they walked, Jimmy enriched Dub with Tappers history and advised him who were the important people to keep happy.

When they approached the front of the building with the executive offices, Dub's hand rubbed the tall, exquisite, ornate front door. "I've never seen such intricate wood carving before," he said.

Jimmy opened the door, revealing a long Oriental rug spanning the length of the marble-floored hallway. Portraits of the Tapperses' ancestors adorned the walls, including the likeness of a highly decorated Confederate soldier.

"Fought with the Confederacy, huh?" Dub asked, pointing to the portrait.

"Grandpa's very proud of his father. He left school at Harvard University in Massachusetts to fight with Robert E. Lee."

"Hmm." Dub shook his head.

Jimmy lowered his voice almost to a whisper, walking Dub from room to room and explaining the cleaning expectations and the executives housed behind each closed door. Each office had a secretary seated in front like a guard warding off uninvited intruders. As Jimmy walked by, the secretaries glanced briefly at Dub as he nodded a greeting to each woman.

After a few minutes of listening and nodding, Dub found himself asking, "Do you mind giving me a pencil and paper? I'd like to take some notes."

"Oh. I forgot you could read and write," Jimmy said. "Certainly, I didn't mean to offend you. Generally, I don't interact with the caretakers here at the company. I'm rotating through the departments and operations at my grandfather's request, to learn this organization from bottom to top. I shouldn't have assumed, as I did, that you couldn't read or write."

"No apology needed, Mr. Jimmy, and I understand. I want to do the best job your grandfather has ever seen from a janitor here at Tappers."

"Dub, I read your file with the letter you received from the company. I now remember it said you could 'read and talk and looked clean and presentable' and that you seemed to be a 'trustworthy Negro to clean the executive offices and supervise four other janitors.' I should've remembered you from that." He asked the nearest secretary for pencil and paper. "I'll pause here for you to write your notes to catch up with the litany of stuff and instructions before we continue."

"Much appreciated," Dub said while jotting his notes. "Thanks, Mr. Jimmy. I'm ready to continue."

Jimmy gave lots of detail on cleaning the executive office. Dub frantically took notes.

The tour ended at the largest and most opulent office with an introduction to Jimmy's grandfather, Jack Tappers. He was a stout yet muscular balding man, over six feet tall with broad shoulders. For someone in a small coal mining town, his attentiveness to detail resonated in his attire. He stood up proudly in a deep-gray herringbone-patterned fitted suit coat with matching vest and pants. Beneath was a stiffly starched blue-striped shirt with a white round club collar, a muted floral necktie, and a white pocket square. His black laced oxford shoes appeared freshly shined.

Stepping around the wooden desk, arms folded, Jack said in a booming voice, "So you're the new man that'll clean my buildings? I heard about you. There's nothing or no one I don't hear about. You're special. Your file indicated you studied books on coal mining, that right?"

"Yes, sir," Dub replied, holding his hat tightly in both hands.

"My men out in the field rejected you for mining work, but you see, I insist on seeing every application. Taking care of my office is like taking care of me. I want the best cooks, cleaners, drivers, and gardeners. These people are personal to me, and rest assured they want to do their best job. It's about trust and integrity, Dublin. You were the best colored man they ever interviewed. I told them to hire you. You're the only janitor allowed in this building, not anyone else on your team. Just you. You're cleaning this office for me and my family. If you do that, we'll take care of you. Are we of one mind here, Dublin?"

"Yes, sir. And please, call me Dub. Everyone does."

"Right." Turning to Jimmy, he said, "Now off you go, Jimmy, and welcome, Dublin . . . I mean Dub." Jack returned to his overstuffed brown leather swivel chair, turning his back on them to continue reading a document.

"Mr. Jimmy, thank you for the tour and introduction. Has Tappers ever had a janitor become a miner?" Dub asked as they walked down the long corridor to the exit.

Jimmy stopped in his tracks and said, "Wow. I don't think so. I mean, I don't think anyone has ever imagined promoting a janitor to mining . . . I mean, I guess it could happen. Never thought about it. There are plenty of coloreds working here as hand loaders and haulers, but I can't think of one in the higher-wage skilled jobs like a machine miner. Those workers generally undercut the coal by machine, which takes quite a bit of skill. They certainly make more money than the janitorial supervisor."

"Do you think that's possible, Mr. Jimmy?"

"I can't promise. What I can say is my grandfather is a straight shooter. He's telling the truth when he says he takes care of the workers that serve our family. He gives those people bonuses at Christmas, and if your family needs something, he helps in various ways. You're in a good job right now."

"I appreciate that, yet there are plenty of opportunities in mining. Isn't that right?"

"We have a lot of Negro workers here. My grandfather said you're strong people and helped prepare the railroad beds and lay the tracks you see here on the campus. After building the foundation of the company, he kept those men here and sent agents out for more men to work inside the hills and underground. I suggest you talk to them about the work. After talking to them, you may change your mind."

"I'll do that, Mr. Jimmy."

"I recently graduated from Harvard, like the other men in my family. It's one of the most prestigious universities in the United States. There are a few students around campus like you, and it opened my eyes to realize that some people like you can go to college too and learn stuff. The ones on my campus came from good families, but they kept to themselves. The way you talk, I see you more like those who went to Harvard."

"I have a brother attending college in Alabama. And a brother working in a mine in West Virginia. Mining is hard work and dangerous. But what does your grandfather believe about my potential to be a miner, Mr. Jimmy?"

"Can't really tell you. If I were a betting man, I'd say he believes you're of more benefit as a janitor. He can trust you. Just don't go striking on him with a union. Listen, I must run, so I'm going to deliver you back to Miss Crenshaw. Let me know how I can help, and I promise to keep track of you, Dub."

The conversation did not dissuade Dub from his mission to impress the Tapperses and become a miner.

***

It took no time for Dub to excel at his new job as a way of elevating himself to a higher paying mining position.

He brought his lunch in the monogramed pail: a fat sandwich stuffed with portions of tender meat and plump soft bread, a bright garden-fresh tomato or piece of fruit, and a jar of sweet tea. It was more appetizing than what Rita offered to the laborers.

Some days Dub walked around while eating his lunch to check his team's work. He made notes of the cleaning problems, recorded the initials of the janitor that produced the inferior work, and tracked each of them down, insisting they go back and redo the cleaning task.

Sometimes he sat at the end of the cafeteria table, eating in silence and looking around to view the Tapperses' table across the room, interacting little with the other janitors. When he did speak, he held a meeting, using lunch time to instruct the men on how to improve their cleaning, alert them to the things he wanted to change, or tell them about complaints from other workers.

Other times he did not have lunch with his crew at all. Instead, he ate lunch with the coal miners in a small metal canteen building near the face of the mine and barraged them with questions.

All his actions as a janitor over the following couple of years had but one purpose—making more money as a coal miner.

CHAPTER 13

COST OF DESIRES
(1924–1925)

Dub's and Tim's lives moved in parallel, each leaving Morriston and Betsey only days apart. The only connection to their departures was a hotel linen laundry bag Mae gifted to Tim for his college travels.

The morning sky cleared after a pouring rain. The air smelled sweet from the petals of flowers torn from their stems emitting their perfume. Birds enjoyed the puddles of water and droplets on the plants. Tim sat on the porch awaiting the sunrise.

His first train ride. Leaving Kate, without even one last look at her in the window. She'd already left town to grow their child in her belly without shame.

Betsey snored inside from another night of intoxication. The loud growls from her throat reminded Tim of a wild animal preparing to attack, like the beatings he'd endured from the broom or whatever weapon was convenient. A brief grin passed his lips, knowing that the growl could be anger that he, Dub, and Zeke had chosen to leave her without a source of income.

Hearing a train in the distance, Tim picked up the laundry bag containing the few clothes and personal items he owned. He tapped his coat pocket. The train ticket bought by Mr. Thomas and the church and the money pouch for the tuition he'd saved stored safely inside. He had thirty minutes to walk to the train station and escape Morriston. His plan remained to one day attend Yale.

After a few hours, and one transfer, he arrived in Talladega, Alabama. A man sat on the platform with a sign that said, "Talladega College." The school had previously sent a letter providing instructions for travel, and Tim waved to the man and introduced himself.

With the two other new students from the same train, he boarded a bus and rode into the foothills of the Blue Ridge Mountains. Tim took in the tall trees and nature surrounding the few buildings that made up the campus.

The escort showed him and the others to an auditorium set up for orientation, where they would receive their housing assignments. Tim had not uttered a word since leaving Morriston, other than to introduce himself to the escort. He stood mesmerized in front of the three-story brick structure topped with a gabled roof. A full-height projecting portico, with four fluted columns supporting the gable, dominated its main facade. The cast-iron balconies on the second and third floor that outlined the auditorium ceiling had no resemblance to Saint John's High School's single-floor structure and exceeded the architecture of the Morriston library.

Tim smiled with satisfaction while sitting at a student desk as instructed to hear the orientation. A white man walked in and paced the room, tapping an ivory-horsehead-topped cane on the floor, stopping to look each student in the face. Tim clenched the sides of the desk.

"I'm your college president," the man said, clasping the cane like a horse whip in both hands. "You were handpicked by me to achieve excellence for your race. By the time you leave here, you'll dispel any stereotypes that my people have of you as descendants of slaves. This is one of the few places you Negroes receive a true liberal arts college education with qualified faculty approaching that of white colleges in New England. Make no mistake. This is a disciplined institution with restrictions and expectations."

"As long as they don't beat me," a man sitting next to Tim mumbled.

The president immediately said, "Pardon me, young man? Did you say something?"

"No, sir. Just cleared my throat."

The president continued. "We don't tolerate violations of the rules. You'll be disciplined, which could mean probation or expulsion. Getting kicked out of this institution will haunt you and end any prospects you have for success. You will attend all your classes every day. Each of you has a job to help defray your tuition and to teach you work ethic. You will labor on this campus as assigned. The dress code in your acceptance letter will be enforced. I trust you have the appropriate clothing. If you want to leave campus, you must apply for permission from my office, including if you want to go home. This is for your protection against people that don't want you here to begin with. Church attendance on Sundays is mandatory. We will inspect your room and your body for cleanliness. No drinking, gambling, or smoking. The list of rules is on the door inside your dormitory room."

He tapped the cane on the floor and walked out the front door. Every head turned and watched him march down the sidewalk, cane swinging, to the grand home built for presidents of the college.

The man sitting next to Tim leaned over and whispered into

Tim's ear, "Is this a plantation but with education? I'm here to become a preacher."

"Maybe, but it's still better than living with my mother. People graduate from here with good jobs," Tim said.

Next, the escort stood and guided the students to meet the dean of the college, who reminded Tim of Mr. Thomas in color and disposition. Expressing care with sternness, he signed Tim up to take English, science, math, history, and a French class. The dean encouraged Tim to join the football team, but Tim was not eager to agree to be battered after years with Betsey.

He isolated himself during his freshman year. The collegiate world encapsulated work, classes, study, and eating. Other than thoughts of Kate, only an occasional game of cards in secret with other students to make extra money connected him to Upper Orchard.

Despite the restrictions, he managed to stay out of trouble. He excelled, particularly in the chemistry portion of the science classes and in French, which he desired to learn for Kate.

During the Christmas holiday trip home, he stole over to Upper Orchard each day but saw no hint of Kate. He habitually searched for notes or other communications from her in the tree hollow, in the tree house, or in the gardeners' shed but found nothing.

***

The summer after his freshman year at Talladega, Tim went to Mr. Larry to ask for his job back at the Benson home in Upper Orchard. Mr. Larry was pleased to have Tim's help with the many summer gatherings the Bensons held for neighbors, friends, and business prospects. He also told Tim about taking the next step with Sadie. They'd married.

One night after working at the Bensons', Tim ventured to Kate's house to view the interior from his place of safety.

Reaching into the tree cavity, he found an envelope with Kate's handwriting.

> Tim, never come here again. Janie Benson gossiped at school that I liked a colored boy because I told her that night when we had dinner at her house. She saw how I looked at you and I told her I thought colored boys were cute. She also told her mother and the word spread to my mother. No one knows you are the one I like. I had to tell my parents that a colored boy fathered my baby because the minute our baby was born, the people in Illinois knew it was a colored child. My daddy believes I was raped and told the police. My family has been shamed and ostracized. My father's business has suffered. He never talks to me, and my mother never touches me. You mustn't be seen here, or you could be killed.
>
> Kindly, Kate

Tim looked across the estate into the parlor window. Kate's face appeared pale and thin. Sadie periodically entered the room to feel her forehead, give her elixirs, reheat the hot water bottle, and adjust the blanket that covered her lethargic body from neck to toe. He locked eyes with Kate while she twined her fingers through the starched white crocheted-lace handkerchief he'd given her on her seventeenth birthday. After a barely perceptible smile, Kate shook her head side to side.

Nevertheless, she continued to sit in the same place each evening before and after dinner, wasting away. After work, he'd exit the door of the grocery store. Turning right took him on the path home and turning left took him to Kate's house. The ritual repeated itself, as each time he made the decision to turn right.

Betsey jumped out of the kitchen chair when she saw Tim coming up the sidewalk to the back stoop.

"I'm glad you're home. I didn't see enough money in the jar. Where's your money?"

"Why, Mama?" he said, stopping short of opening the screen door.

"Why? Because I got a leaky roof." She walked up to the screen door. "Those arrogant bastards, Dub and Zeke, don't send me nothing, and they're the ones making the most money."

"Stop your lies. Zeke sends you money almost every week. You just drink it all away. I can smell it through the door."

"You ungrateful—"

He looked behind Betsey.

With balled fists and spread legs, he barked, "Who's that?"

"Just Mr. Algee. He looked at the roof. How much are you making up at that store and being a houseboy for those rich people this summer?"

"I'll see you later, Mama. I can't stand the foul odor coming from the house right now."

With only a thin wood-framed screen door separating mother and son, Tim turned to go back down the stairs of the stoop. Fists still clenched, he mumbled incoherently between his teeth.

"Tim, you come back here."

In one smooth motion Betsey pushed the door open with her right hand. The screen-door spring hinge suddenly creaked and snapped, separating from the door. The back of the door smacked against the house as she grabbed the broom that lay against the porch wall with her left. Tim did not turn to see the commotion behind him.

"Betsey, stop. Don't hurt the boy," Mr. Algee said, running from the house to catch her.

The snapping sound of the wooden handle splitting in half and the sound of the wood against Tim's skull blended as one.

"You're going to kill him."

Mr. Algee grabbed Betsey around her waist, lifting her feet off the ground. Her arms flailed.

"Get your goddamn hands off me. I'm going to kill that yellow bastard child. He's nothing but the devil," she said, reaching back to grab Mr. Algee's head. They both fell to the ground. "I'll kill you too, Algee."

Mr. Algee sat on top of Betsey, securing her hands above her head.

"Stop, Algee! Get off me. You're hurting me."

Mr. Algee lifted Betsey by her waist and struggled to carry her back into the house. Sounds of furniture falling and bodies hitting walls resounded from inside the home.

Tim opened his eyes, not aware how long he had been unconscious. He knelt on the ground, feeling the large lump and an open wound on the back of his head, gauging the latest gravity of Betsey's cruelty. Blood dripped down the waves in his hair, falling onto the starched white shirt.

"Whatever he's doing, you deserve it! You won't make me cry, Mama!" Tim screamed.

Finally, the sounds stopped when Algee sat Betsey in a living room chair and offered her a shot of whiskey from his flask. There they continued talking about how to repair the roof.

In the days that followed, Tim suffered severe headaches and blurred vision, and Betsey continued monitoring the coins in the jar.

The next evening after work, he headed left, walking slowly, wary of being seen by the police or neighbors. Tucked behind the tree, he agonized as Kate stumbled feebly to the chair, sat down, and stared out the window with a weak smile. The outline of his body made a halo in the lights beaming from the house. He gazed while Kate's eyelids slowly lowered.

In a soft voice he said, "Kate, I will graduate from Yale. I promise. Then I'll take you and our baby to France. I'll become rich and we'll go on a boat cruise around the world to all the continents."

Hands gracefully folded in her lap on top of the handkerchief, her face pointed toward the window. He saw Kate's lips move, appearing to say "Go," and then she closed her eyes.

Kate never moved again. Tim stood motionless; in shock after witnessing the death of his dear friend and love.

Movement inside the parlor startled him. Sadie walked in with a tray of food. Seeing Kate's hands limp in her lap, and her head slumped to the side, she dropped the tray. Kate's mother screamed upon hearing dishes crash to the floor and ran to her, and her father lifted the girl's lifeless body out of the chair. The mother smacked Kate's face, yet nothing reconnected her with the world.

Tim struggled, pacing, then stepped toward the window, but darted back into the shadows when someone looked in his direction. He crouched down against the tree, watching the family run frantically throughout the house. The doctor arrived. He carried Kate's body away, the servants lowered the curtains throughout the entire house, and the show ended. Tim sat while the Russos turned off all the lights, then walked home.

Two days later, the family published Kate's obituary in the paper with no mention of a baby and no mention of how she died, just the date: July 12, 1925. Tim followed Kate's body to the back door of the funeral home. Vigilantly he sat outside until they placed the casket in the hearse to drive her home for viewing by family and friends.

During those days, he stood under the walnut tree in the same manner he had during her life. Sadie stood in the parlor late one night, holding a baby at Kate's coffin. Tim's eyes locked onto the baby, briefly admiring the serene and beautiful olive-skinned face, big round eyes, and rosy cheeks. The baby smiled.

On the day of Kate's burial, from far away, he followed the funeral procession of cars. He remained invisible to those in attendance, standing at a distance outside the church. Despondent, he witnessed the white casket carried in by six pallbearers, topped with a carpet of pink and white roses.

After a short service, the coffin was carried from the church in the same manner, followed by a line of people of all ages. The casket floated down the street on a horse-drawn carriage, surrounded by a full garden of flowers.

He ran to the cemetery and grieved from afar, watching the family cry by Kate's grave as they lowered the white glistening coffin into the ground. He cried too, stifling himself.

People filed away from the cemetery and the sun went down. He walked to Kate's grave, covered with fresh dirt, and threw his body on the ground. Pressing himself into the dirt, he clutched at the rose petals from the floral carpet draped across her grave. Stuffing a handful in his pocket, he fell asleep from exhaustion. The sound of an owl startled him awake. Touching his face, his hand came away covered in mud from the stream of tears flooding from his eyes.

The baby, Tim thought. *That wasn't Sadie's baby. Mr. Larry said he and Sadie married, but that baby didn't look like either one of them.*

He leaped up and ran home in the darkness. Quietly tiptoeing through the back door to the writing desk in the kitchen, he removed paper and pencil from the drawer, then closed his eyes to envision the infant. He continued sketching as a picture emerged of the baby's likeness. Silently walking to the bed once shared with his brothers, he reached beneath the mattress and removed the cigar box. He delicately folded the picture and then placed it on top of Kate's previous notes, along with the rose petals.

CHAPTER 14

PROMISES (1925–1926)

Determined to fulfill his promise to Kate, Tim returned to Talladega for his sophomore year; registered for the second level of liberal arts courses in the sciences, English, math, and French; and poured himself into academia, eschewing the other privileges and amenities of being a smart and attractive young man.

The thought of friendship never crossed his mind, and he ignored all signs that his six-foot height and trim look attracted women. Whether in class or walking across campus, female students pointed, huddled, and discussed the mysterious man who did not speak to anyone volitionally. Male students sought to befriend him, but unless they invited him to play a prohibited game of cards for money, Tim returned to studying and work.

A separate building roomed the girls and stayed under the watchful eye of a housemother. The campus rules for the genders to socialize allowed only three occasions. One in class, another in church, and the last, walking on campus. Even then, speaking with a person of the opposite sex drew scrutiny.

A freshman female student from Morriston sought out Tim at the recommendation of Mr. Thomas. Being a freshman, she did not have the same classes as Tim. One laboratory instructed students who wanted to further their studies in chemistry and biology in preparation for nursing, pharmacy, or medicine. The freshman student orchestrated a chance meeting in the hallway to the laboratory where they both attended science classes.

The woman dropped her books in front of Tim as he exited the laboratory, forcing him to stop and assist with picking them up. The attractive petite young woman, at barely over five feet tall, had flawless caramel-brown skin, deep-brown eyes, and tightly curled hair pulled back in a stylish bun. Her dress conformed to the college uniform of a long gray skirt, white blouse, and black leather shoes. As they knelt on the floor, she looked up at him and smiled. Tim kept his eyes focused on the floor while courteously retrieving a mathematics book and English book, handing them to her one at a time.

They both reached for the nursing book at the same time, but Tim pulled it from her hand, stood, and opened it. He did not respond to the young woman who stood up smiling and glancing at him with the hope they would exchange a few words. Tim fanned the pages and stopped at a page that described anesthesia using organic materials. One described the use of fermented raw eggs captured in a glass jar as a potent inhalant that made people faint. The young woman continued to wait patiently while Tim read several pages to the end of the chapter. He closed the book, studied the cover again, and handed it to the young woman.

"Thank you—" she said softly, looking directly at him while blushing.

He nodded and turned to leave.

"—Tim." She abruptly said his name and stood in place watching him.

He stopped, turned to look in her direction.

"I'm Freda. Mr. Thomas told me to meet you. I just graduated from Saint John's High School. I remember you and your mother from Low Orchard. We lived a couple of blocks away, near where your brother Dub lived before he moved."

Tim struggled to reply. "Low Orchard? Yes. Nice meeting you, Freda." He immediately turned and sprinted to his French class.

The young woman froze in the hallway, watching as Tim descended the stairwell. Rushing feet echoed down the hallway of the tiled floor below. Seconds later his hands slammed the wood door as he quickly exited the building. They never spoke again.

***

Over the course of the school year, he earned straight As.

The trek across campus to the dean's office took several minutes. Running up the steps to the third floor two at a time, he had one final task to perform before the summer.

The last door in the dimly lit hallway had the word "Dean" etched in the glass. Tim used one knuckle to knock on the window. No answer. He knocked a little harder with three knuckles, then received the response, "Come in."

Timidly opening the door, he said, "Sir?"

"Yes?" said the dean.

"My name is Timothy Brisco."

"Ah. Mr. Brisco. Second-year student, right? And what can I do for you?"

"I want to talk about transferring to another university. You see, I have an A average across all my classes so far."

"Yes. I'm familiar with you. Let me pull out your file. And while I do, tell me why you want to leave Talladega and where it is you want to go."

"Yale, sir."

"Excuse me?" The dean paused and chuckled as he pulled out a brown file with Tim's name on the top.

"Yale. Sir."

"And why Yale?"

"It's not a good school?"

"Oh, it's an excellent school. I don't challenge the choice. I've never had a student from Talladega ask about Yale, and Negroes aren't typically admitted to Yale. You still have not told me why you want to leave here."

"I promised a friend I would go to Yale."

"Is that friend at Yale?"

"No, sir."

"So why would they encourage you to attend Yale?"

"Look, please. I just need to go to Yale. I told you the reason."

"Settle down. No more questions. Just one thing. You're doing very well here. At this rate you are bound to graduate and move on to better things. I was told by your chemistry teacher that you could be a doctor, pharmacist, or scientist, the way you handle yourself in the laboratory. You have a very remote chance of admission into Yale. And I'm telling you, if you are admitted, they'll make no effort to keep you there. As a matter of fact, they may push you to fail. But if this is really what you want, I'll help."

"This is what I want."

"All right. Well then, if Yale does not work out, for any reason, we'd love to have you complete your studies here. From your file and speaking with the faculty, I know you've been an outstanding student. I'll request an application to Yale and help you complete it."

The completed application was sent to Yale before Tim left campus for the summer. During the weeks leading up to the train ride home, his pencil poised each day above a sheet of paper to write a letter alerting Betsey to the end of the semester and his return home. The writing utensil shook between his fingers, drawing illegible figures. Sweat beaded on his forehead until he banged his fist on the desk and tossed the paper into the trash, forestalling the notice of his arrival.

On the short train ride home, he periodically rubbed his eyes, shutting them tight and opening them, to clear the blurring. Scars on his forearms from Betsey's drunken assaults the previous year demanded his visual attention more and more the closer the train drew to Morriston.

The house was quiet. He arrived close to lunchtime, and Betsey was not in any of her typical spots on the back or front porch. No scent of bread, meat, or vegetables flowed from the kitchen. No voices chatting inside. He made a tentative approach into the house, looking side to side into each room of the small bungalow.

Betsey's door stood slightly open. His expression grew more guarded the closer he got to the bedroom. He pushed the door open gingerly until he saw her bare feet hanging off the bed, beyond the floral quilt made by the church ladies. Betsey lay fully clothed, dress askew, mouth open and snoring. An empty liquor bottle had fallen from her hand and lay in a wet spot on the quilt.

Tim turned, placed the laundry bag with his belongings in his bedroom, and walked to the cemetery. A white marble angel now stood in the spot where he'd lain prone in the dirt the night of Kate's burial. The angel's wings spread wide, casting a shadow across Kate's grave. Grass covered the dirt that his tears had moistened that previous summer. Her name and the two dates beneath it told nothing of how or why she had died. He sat down on the iron bench at the foot of her resting place and told her about his accomplishments in school and his application to Yale. He again promised to graduate from Yale, become rich, find the baby in his drawing, and fulfill all their dreams of traveling around the world.

"We'll celebrate my admission to Yale the next time I come back."

Tim strolled to the grocery store to secure the part-time job he had held since first moving to Morriston, then made his way to Upper Orchard. Nothing had changed except the small children, who had grown a few inches. The landscaping had changed at some of the homes to reflect the preferences of new homeowners, and fancier cars marked the growing wealth.

Kate's home looked no different. The only change on the estate was to the pale and abandoned tree house. The wooden frame, no longer pristine, now revealed weather-worn planks slowly merging into the tree branches. The window revealed the top of the desk where Kate had first viewed him under the walnut tree. Curtains fluttered in and out of the windows as if beckoning Tim to climb inside one last time.

Mrs. Russo opened the front door with an inquisitive look at Tim standing on the sidewalk. Sticking his hands in his pockets, he sauntered away. She closed the door and locked it.

As he entered the Benson estate, the gardener attending the rose bushes waved and smiled. "Home for the summer, huh, Tim? Good to see you. How's school? I should start calling you Doctor."

"Nah, not yet. But I'm an honor student with high marks in my classes. I'm thinking about pharmacy."

Tim waved at other workers while walking up the long path to the back and into the kitchen, where the cook pensively stirred a pot of soup. Tim stood at the kitchen table breathing deeply, and his body visibly relaxed. He turned around, looking at the door separating the kitchen from the dining room.

"Where's Mr. Larry?"

"Oh my goodness, Tim. I didn't see you. Welcome back. How long have you been standing there?"

"Not long. I was—"

"And who are you, young man," said a man dressed in a butler's uniform. "Miss Sarah, friends are not allowed back here at any time."

"Tim is not a friend. Well, I guess he is sort of a friend, but he works here in the summertime when he's off from school. He goes to Talladega, the Negro college. Now that Mr. Larry is gone, you must put him back to work. Tim, this here is Mr. David. He replaced Mr. Larry."

"Oh," Mr. David said. "So the Bensons are aware of this?"

"Yes," Miss Sarah said. "They expect you to hire him. They like him especially because they have more parties in the summer and you'll need the extra hands. He knows what to do." Sarah winked at Tim.

Mr. David nodded, scrutinizing Tim from head to toe. "Tim, you come back tomorrow. I'll talk to Mrs. Benson for approval."

"Sure," Tim said. "Just so you know, I work at the grocery store during the day and then come here before dinnertime and work until night. I have the shoes, suit, and shirts Mrs. Benson requires. Miss Sarah, where did Mr. Larry go?"

"You remember he was dating a lady named Sadie and they married? She worked in a house around the way as a nanny for a girl named Kate. Well, Kate died. You may remember her? They came here for dinner one night. I was told she looked at you pretty hard. Well, anyhow, Sadie looked after her when the girl got sick and died. According to Larry, Sadie became very sad because she took care of that girl from the day she was born, and when she died, they up and moved north out of Alabama. He got a job at some coal mine. Lots of our men are leaving the South and doing that."

"I have two brothers working at mines. I guess they make lots of money."

"Well, Tim, you stay in college. You're not the type to get your hands dirty. You do something with your brain."

***

Tim settled into his summer routine, seven days a week. Sunup, to the grocery store. Late afternoon, turn left to the Bensons' in Upper Orchard. Late at night, cloister away in the bedroom to avoid Betsey. Hope for good news from Yale.

Then, early August, the news came. *The Admissions Office has completed its evaluation of this year's candidates, and I write with sincere regret to say that we are not able to offer you a place in the class starting Fall 1926.* One sheet of paper. One sentence.

"Tim! The jar doesn't have enough money."

Walking wide legged from the kitchen to avoid tripping over her own feet, Betsey slowly navigated down the hallway, dressed in the same clothes she'd worn the past two days. Stains from food, liquor, and sweat from the August heat weighed down the fabric of the cotton floral housedress. The oils from unwashed hair plastered the strands to her scalp. Through it all, she managed to cook three meals a day and clean the house. Reaching his bedroom, she leaned her head on the door and braced herself within the door jamb.

The locked door rattled on the hinges. He grimaced. "Dammit," he whispered, hitting his fists against the pillow where the letter lay.

"Tim! You hear me, boy. What've you been doing with your money? We need stuff in this house. It costs me to feed you. You act like I owe you something. Word on the street is Dub is making big money and can't even send me anything. I might as well find a roomer and kick your lazy ass out. Come out here, boy. Don't make me bust in there and pull you out."

Tim covered his ears and screamed into the pillow. His head throbbed with pain. "You lowlife bitch," he mumbled to himself. He jumped up and paced the floor like a caged animal. Sweat dripped down his forehead to merge with the tears running from his eyes. Thoughts raced through his head. *I gotta leave this place. How do I get to France? How do I find my baby? How can I make the dream that Kate had for us? I should have known they wouldn't let a colored in that school. I'm a nothing to Yale. A nothing to anybody. I forgot. I'm invisible.*

He crumpled the letter, threw it on the floor, and stomped until the paper absorbed the black rubber from the bottom of the soles. Stopping suddenly, he looked around the room like a prisoner, frantically unlocked the door, pushed Betsey to the wall, and stormed out of the house to work.

The temperature in Morriston reached over ninety degrees. The Bensons and their guests retired to the large wraparound porch of the white antebellum home. Tim went back and forth between the kitchen and serving cold beverages and port wine to guests from Canada who spoke French. He lingered each time.

"*Bonsoir, madame, puis-je vous offrir un verre?*" Tim said to the ladies.

"*Ah! Puis-je avoir un thé glacé s'il vous plaît,*" a guest said with raised eyebrows.

"*Oui, madame,*" Tim said, bowing and nodding. He turned to Mrs. Benson, asking, "What can I get for you, ma'am?"

Mrs. Benson sat speechless for a moment, then replied, "Sweet tea."

After the guests departed, Mrs. Benson rang the bell to request Tim's presence in the parlor and then expressed her surprise and curiosity at how he knew French so well. Walking home from the Bensons', he recited sentences in French, letting out an occasional chuckle.

Arriving home to a quiet house, Tim noticed Betsey was nowhere in sight. Tim went directly to his room and bolted the door. Flopping down on the bed exhausted, he noticed the crumpled letter from Yale had been smoothed out and was now prominently displayed face up on his dresser.

The next day, he reported for work at the Bensons' as usual.

"Tim, a letter was left for you on the kitchen table. Some little boy from the hotel brought it over."

After reading it, expressionless, Tim tucked it in his pocket and continued working. Crossing the tracks into Low Orchard that night, the sounds of a jazz trio radiated from the tavern. He relaxed at the bar, absorbing the soothing music. Another hot night drew neighbors, people from church, and old classmates outside with their glasses of beer and liquor. Typically, Tim would walk past, but the vibrant activity in the street pulled him in. He strolled to the bar and asked for a glass of Scotch with ice. The first swallow soothed his thoughts. He opened the letter again, contemplating its contents. The rest of the Scotch went down much easier.

Several hours later, his arrival at Betsey's proved disruptive.

"Boy, don't come in my house when you're plastered. I won't stand for it. You need to get the hell out of here," Betsey screamed.

"And who the hell are you to tell me about drinking? You walk around the neighborhood like a boozy whore."

"Get out! Nobody insults me in my own home. You have no idea what I've been through for you kids. Watching your daddy die. He left me with this mess. All my life I sacrificed my body for everybody. Now I can do what I damn well please and don't need to take shit from you. Just leave me some money and go back to that school that's making you think you're better than the rest of us with your proper talk. Ha! You even got rejected by Yale, whatever that is."

"You're right, Talladega didn't make me better. It couldn't get me to Yale, so I'm done with Talladega. But it did do one thing useful. It taught me French. I have the chance to make my way to France, where I'll be respected and rich. That's what Kate told me. I'll always be invisible. I'll never be anything more if I'm tied to Green Creek and to you. Look at me! I'm not Tuttle's son. Look at my skin. I'm not brown. Look at my hair. It's not frizzy or kinky. Look at my eyes. They have specks of brown and green. I look whiter than you. But in this country, I'm stuck because I'm your son. Now, Mother dear, I'm going far away where none of this matters."

He pulled the letter from his pocket, waving it around the room. "I'm not the son of a brown indentured servant or a stinking drunk." He pinched his nose and scrunched up his face.

Betsey leaned into Tim's face. "Yeah? Well, you're the son of a rapist. How's that any better? Does Kate know that—whoever she is?" Droplets of Betsey's spit speckled across his face.

He grabbed Betsey's throat and pressed her against the wall. Struggling to breathe, she pulled at Tim's hands, digging her nails into his wrists. "Don't you ever let Kate's name cross your ugly lips," he hissed.

Tim tossed Betsey to the floor and stumbled back to his bedroom, rubbing his eyes to clear his vision. After it returned to normal, he grabbed the cigar box containing the notes from Kate and the drawing of the baby and walked out.

Muttering, he said, "I need to leave here to stop this pain in my head." He stepped over Betsey, still lying where she'd landed, and turned and spit at her feet.

That night, clouds covered the moon. Tim made his way to the cemetery in the darkness, where he spent the night sharing his life plans with the white marble angel manifesting itself as Kate. He shared the picture of the baby and his desire to find their child.

"I failed, Kate. I promised to celebrate my admission to Yale the next time I came back."

Kate's voice said, "I told you. Yale is very selective." She went on to lecture him, telling him to remember how her parents really wanted her to be with a wealthy, educated man from Yale. Why? He knew why—to continue the lifestyle they gave her or even better. "I want us to be together," she said. "But we must live in another country, like France." He listened as she explained that there, they would be fully accepted and could cruise around the world.

He held the cigar box to his chest. "I'll do whatever it takes for me, you, and our baby to be together."

The following morning, Betsey sent a telegram to Zeke. Wire money to buy Tim a train ticket. Sending him to Dub's house. Tim beat me and is dropping out of school. That evening she sent a letter addressed to Dub and Mae.

> Tim has been drinking and belligerent, and he choked me. He told me he is not returning to Talladega for his junior year. Zeke sent me money to buy Tim a one-way train ticket to Abingdon, hoping Tim would be influenced by your prosperity to get his own life on track. I hope this letter reaches you before he does. If all goes as it should, you will see him soon.

CHAPTER 15

AMBITION (1926)

Dub stayed focused on advancing at Tappers with no inquiries into the family he'd left behind in Alabama, offering no financial support and seeking no knowledge of their difficulties. The janitorial team expanded and became more disciplined under his leadership. He built relationships with the mining supervisors and everyone who worked in the executive office and became a favorite of Jack Tappers's.

But neither his team nor Rita prepared him for the shift in atmosphere taking place at Tappers. As he entered the cafeteria, he made mental notes of the substandard cleaning done by his team. Approaching the table where his crew typically sat, he paused, noticing empty seats. The other employees did not converse as usual. Looking around, he first saw one of the janitors, Jeremiah, sitting alone at a table on the opposite side of the room in the first row of tables where the Tappers family and their executives gathered. He saw another janitor, Bootsie, occupying a table in the second row, also alone, where white workers usually ate lunch.

Dub froze, looking at Jeremiah and Bootsie. A voice that he had not heard since the interviews in Morriston emerged from the silence.

"You belong at the other table, over there," said the slick, sandy-red-haired man, approaching Jeremiah. He gave off a menacing presence with his height and breadth that towered over Jeremiah's head. "Move it."

The kitchen workers paused their tasks to listen. No cooking sounds or noise of clattering pots and pans floated across the room as usual. Sandy-Red turned to Dub and beamed his focus directly toward him.

"Mister smart-man supervisor, you need to come and straighten out your boys before this becomes your problem."

Dub approached Jeremiah and laid his hand on Jeremiah's shoulder. He said, "Let's go."

Jeremiah, who had been casually eating his lunch with his head lowered and eyes focused on his food, slowly turned to look up at Dub. Their eyes locked. Dub nodded silently toward the other side of the room with pleading eyes. He moved his hand beneath Jeremiah's armpit, pulling him upright. Jeremiah stood reluctantly, without breaking his gaze at Dub, picked up his lunch, and started walking out of the building. The other janitor, Bootsie, did the same, following Dub and Jeremiah.

Once outside, Dub said, "What's wrong with you two? I can't have my men making a mess like this! We've got good jobs and I'm not about to lose mine over the likes of you. Jack Tappers has been good to us, and he trusts us with his property. Don't go messing this up. They don't like striking here, and the whites don't want to eat with the coloreds. What're you going to do if they kick you out? There's a line of other men who want your job."

"Who are you talking about, Dub? Us or yourself?" Jeremiah asked. "Jack Tappers never did a damn thing for me. I've never talked to the man. I don't care about losing my job. I got my farm I can work. You're thinking about your own ass, boss."

"Man, I'm tired of looking at their hot food while we are served cold sandwiches," Bootsie said. "I'm tired of you making us go over our work time and time again because you're scared of them Tappers men like they're slave masters. You don't know diddly-squat about me as a person. You only want to talk about work, like you're a slave driver too. The only respect and conversation you offer is when I cut your hair out there behind the miners' canteen."

"Bootsie, the old man Tappers already knows what happened in there," Dub said. "And like I said, I'm not having it. I didn't move my family up here to start trouble. Now go back to work, and I better not see you pull some crap like that again."

No more words passed between the three men.

The next morning, when Dub stepped onto his back porch to leave for work, he saw a note tacked to the door reading, *UNCLE TOM, WATCH YOURSELF AND YOUR FAMILY.*

Who left this? he thought. *What am I supposed to do with this?* After staring at the words for several seconds, he nodded and said out loud to himself, "Don't do anything, Dub. Pretend you didn't see it. If you're going to survive and do well here, keep your head down."

After receiving the note, he started a practice of waking up shortly after midnight and walking the perimeter around his house. With increased frequency, he received letters written in pencil and capital letters wishing harm to his family and home. Voodoo dolls appeared on the back porch.

For weeks after Jeremiah and Bootsie ate at the first and second rows of tables in protest of the segregated cafeteria, all the janitors started eating with the coal miners in the metal canteen building near the face of the mine, leaving Dub to eat alone at their usual table in the cafeteria. The cooks continued to serve Dub when he asked, yet extended few other courtesies to him. The janitors and cooks whispered among themselves or stopped talking when Dub walked into a room. He found wastebaskets spilled on the floor, and worse, feces smeared on a bathroom wall. His team denied culpability or knowledge, while chuckling behind his back and other times expressing vile hostilities.

Dub persisted in cleaning every corner of Tappers meticulously and walked around the facilities to assure top-notch quality. If anyone became defiant, he threatened to report them to his boss. But he continued to supervise his team as normal and did not participate in the protest to integrate the cafeteria.

***

One morning, seven days later, Dub jogged through the entrance to Tappers during a rainstorm.

"Dub, my grandfather wants to talk to you as soon as possible," said Jimmy, dressed in a brown wool suit and tie, standing beneath a large black umbrella.

During the past year, Jimmy had become vice president of mining operations. Since Dub's first day at Tappers, without saying anything about it, Jimmy had taken it upon himself to informally provide Dub with educational information on coal mining and inform him of the changes in miner staffing. He also sought Dub out to see if he had any questions about the goings-on at Tappers and made sure he knew about anything impacting his job and team. Dub knew not to press Jimmy about ever becoming a coal miner but expressed his appreciation for the education and information.

"Yes, sir. Right away," Dub said.

Jimmy shifted his umbrella to cover Dub too and led him into the executive offices. The hallway appeared longer than usual. Dub glanced at each secretary's face as he passed. None looked back at him, focused on their papers, typewriters, and phones. Located at the end of the corridor, Jack's double-doored office remained closed all day unless permission to enter was granted by his secretary.

She lifted the phone when she heard Jimmy's steady footsteps and said, "He's here."

Neither man spoke until Jimmy opened the door to his grandfather's office, revealing Jack Tappers in the large brown swivel chair, staring out the window at the campus.

"Grandfather, Dub is here," Jimmy said.

The air of formality permeated throughout Jack's office. The scent of cleaning products awakened every sense. Shiny wood surfaces glowed despite the dark rain clouds hiding the sun. Not a speck of lint existed in the tightly woven pashmina wool carpet imported from India. A spotless window offered no distinction between indoors and outdoors. Even the outsides of the wastebaskets were as stain-free and pristine as if they were brand new.

Dub and Jimmy waited in silence. Dub stood in the threshold breathing heavily. Clutching his hat tightly between both hands, his eyes expanded, taking in the scene that represented his work at Tappers. Sweat seeped through his shirt. He fought back the tears that began to rim his eyes. The crunched hatband absorbed the tension from his body.

Jack continued watching workers coming and going on the grounds of the mining company during shift change, the smoke rising from stacks, and the coal dumping into train cars. The steam whistle blared, signaling the start of the morning crew. He nodded and grinned.

"Dub," Mr. Tappers said, spinning around, walking to the front of the desk, and placing his hands in his pockets. "Glad to see you. Come in. Sit down. Let's talk."

Dub followed Jimmy into the office. Jimmy immediately pointed to a chair next to the door. Dub stopped and sat erect on the edge of the seat. The hat remained clenched in his hands, and his elbows squeezed into his waist to hide the sweat that now ran down his sides. Jimmy proceeded farther into the office, stood next to Jack, and crossed his arms.

Jack cleared his throat. "You're doing a fantastic job taking care of this place. I couldn't be happier."

Dub's hands suddenly loosened, and his back dared to slightly relax. A brief smile passed his lips.

"Thank you, sir," he said nervously.

Mr. Tappers paused to balance himself on the front corner of the large desk. Pointing at Dub, he said, "Jimmy told me coal mining is in your blood. I'm willing to try it out if that's what you want. Jimmy says you're ready. But I'm worried about one thing, though," he said, touching the pointer finger to his lips. "It came to my attention that unnecessary friction is growing about who sits where in the cafeteria. Dub, the world is the way it is and neither you nor I can, or should, do much about that. Be comfortable with your station here, I say."

Dub nodded.

"I appreciate you've been a leader and have shown people how to behave in the cafeteria, at the risk of being called an Uncle Tom and being intimidated," Jack said. "Oh yes, I know about that. Not much goes on around here that doesn't make its way to my ears. Don't be embarrassed. I'm proud you risked that type of humiliation with your team. You put your head down and kept working as you should. Jimmy tells me you keep your men in line and don't make trouble. You're a Tappers man."

"Thank you for saying so, sir," Dub said.

Jack nodded. "I'm giving you a raise. Now, I'm going to pay you more than I've been paying other coloreds coming up from the South because you're a smart one. Jimmy said you have a brother in college too. Most of your people, the coloreds, are loaders in the mines, and some do picking. But because you're different and seem to come from a good family and have done well by me, we want to try you out as a machine miner. Right, Jimmy?"

"Right," Jimmy said. "We bought some new mining equipment and I want you as an operator. But before that, you'll do some basic underground training as a pick miner and learn a little about cutting, drilling, and blasting. You'll report to the personnel office Monday morning. We assigned a trusted miner, Keenan, to train you. You can tell your team today. Tell them we are promoting a worker from our estate to your job. None of your workers deserve a promotion to supervisor."

"But don't go telling them your wage," Jack said, wagging his finger at Dub. "I need you to keep working hard and encourage the others who want to make a statement, like joining the union or striking, that they should follow your example instead. I may make you a mining crew supervisor quickly if you handle this well. Now work your magic for me, Dub."

With that, Mr. Tappers stood and turned around to look out the window once more. He nodded and waved at the long-legged, broad-shouldered security guard with thick curly hair who was always riding a horse. The man tipped his wide-brimmed hat to Jack perched commandingly in the expansive office window.

"Thank you, sir. You can count on me," Dub said.

Feeling Jimmy touch his shoulder, Dub rose and left the room.

After closing the door, Jimmy said, "I told you. See there? Your ambition has been rewarded. Others will see that too."

"Thank you, Mr. Jimmy. I'm grateful to you too. May I shake your hand?"

"Ah . . . certainly," he said, quickly clasping and releasing Dub's hand. "Well, I'll be seeing you around." Jimmy swiftly turned and retreated to Jack's office.

Dub went about his morning with increased fever and intensity, barking orders at the janitorial team. At lunch, he convened the crew in the cafeteria and announced his promotion to the mines.

"So that's your reward for keeping us in line?" Jeremiah said.

"Yep. You know it," Bootsie said, laughing and slapping Jeremiah's back.

"Look at this place," Dub said. "It's immaculate. I did my job."

"OK. So, who takes your place? Are they giving it to one of us?"

"No. someone from the Tappers estate. Monday, they start."

"Another Dub Brisco," Bootsie said, chuckling again.

Dub picked up his lunch and left the building. The security guard on the horse nodded at Dub and gave him a half smile. Dub continued walking up the road to a vista of the mine, where he leaned against a wall and ate his apple, much as he'd done at the factory in Morriston, allowing himself to feel the glow of success.

When he went home, he waved to the children playing in the yard.

"Where's your mom?" he said to Matthew.

"She's in the kitchen. She told us to stay out here while she finishes the pie. I'm stuck here watching Genese, Calvin, and Chloe. I'm sure dinner is ready because she called Bernie and Amaya inside to help set the table."

He yanked off his hat and sprung up the four steps, taking them two at a time, onto the back porch.

"Mae. Mae, I got something to tell you."

"I'm right here in the kitchen. Don't yell, I'm putting a pie in the oven. Dinner is ready. What is it you need to tell me?"

Hearing Dub enlivened eight-year-old Bernie's and six-year-old Amaya's interest. They dawdled preparing the table to eavesdrop on their father's announcement.

"Girls, go outside and play until we call you," he said, shooing them away with his hand.

Bernie pouted and sauntered out the door with Amaya reluctantly following.

Dub grabbed Mae's waist. "You're looking at a coal machine miner," he said. "Mr. Jack Tappers told me himself. Can you believe it? I'll be making more than any other Negro miner coming up from the South. He may make me a mining crew supervisor if I do well. It's all happening as we planned, Mae."

Mae screamed and hugged him. "I'm so happy. Can I give you my list of things we need for the house? Oh my, our dreams are coming true. This was all worth it."

They both looked at each other smiling.

Her smile quickly disappeared.

"What's the matter?" Dub said, his grin quickly fading.

"Oh my. I need to tell you something. A letter came from your mother addressed to both of us. It's about Tim."

"What about him?"

"I'll show you the letter, but it said he isn't doing well."

"I'm not surprised. When I went to tell Mama and Tim we were moving to Abingdon, he told me he was in love with some girl named Kate and she was pregnant. He needs to get over it. Doesn't he realize the opportunity he has, Mae? All this crying and mess over a girl."

"Well, the letter said he's drinking, belligerent, and choked Betsey. He's not returning to college for his third year. I hate to say it, but this sounds like something your mother instigated."

Dub raised his voice. "Mae, don't start with me."

Dub hung his hat on a hook behind the kitchen door and leaned against the wall with folded arms and head bent to examine his shoes.

"I never told you this, but Tim came over to our house in Morriston the night before we left for Abingdon," Mae said. "I had no idea he was drinking until he lifted his face. His eyes were half-closed, and he slurred his words. I sat on the porch with him. Tears ran down his face and he held his head between his knees. He blubbered, 'I love her.' I had no idea what he was talking about. I should have told you, but things were going so well for us, I didn't want to involve myself in Tim's and Betsey's messes. But, since he was going to college, all I did was give him one of the extra laundry bags to pack his stuff."

Dub looked up, shaking his head. "I'm glad you didn't tell me, because I told him I didn't have time for his problems or my mother's drama. Tim needs to deal with his life like I deal with mine."

He walked over to Mae and gave her a kiss on the cheek. "Mae, look, I want to relax and enjoy dinner. What're we going to do? We can't get distracted with Betsey's and Tim's problems. We gotta stay focused on our own progress. What else does the letter say?"

Dub walked to the kitchen sink and vigorously washed his hands.

"Well, I'll read the entire thing to you." Mae reached into her apron pocket and pulled out the letter. "It says, 'Tim has been drinking and belligerent, and he choked me. He told me he is not returning to Talladega for his junior year. Zeke sent me money to buy Tim a one-way train ticket to Abingdon, hoping Tim would be influenced by your prosperity to get his own life on track. I hope this letter reaches you before he does. If all goes as it should, you will see him soon.'"

Dub raised his voice again. "I don't want a damn thing to do with him if he's beating up on Mama. And dropping out of college? He's throwing away an opportunity to move up in life. The ingrate. And what the hell is Mama thinking sending him here without asking. I have no time or room for him here. I don't want him here ruining our reputation. Especially now that I'm moving up in the company."

"Well, the letter says he's on his way. So if we must take him, then I don't want you spending any of our money on him. Just put him in the storage barn or shack out back. And make sure he stays away from me and the kids if he's drinking alcohol. I refuse to have him influencing the children."

"Good idea. He can stay out there and be a ghost. Beating up Mama. Drunkenness. Lack of ambition. Whining over some girl. He's on his own. I'm through with him."

Dub did not give Betsey's letter another thought.

CHAPTER 16

THE TICKET (1926)

Betsey moved swiftly around the kitchen; with precision, she placed a dinner plate in front of Tim. With the same zeal, she cleaned the entire room. Amid all the noise and activity, she told Tim about the train ticket to Abingdon, Illinois, that he was going to live with Dub. Never looking at her son, and leaving no time for a reply, she left for a gathering at the speakeasy.

The kitchen was devoid of life. Tim stared at the stove, one hand holding a fork and the other a knife. Reluctantly, he began to eat. When done, Tim retired to his bedroom, locking the door.

Neither Tim nor Betsey discussed the vicious words and physical attack two nights earlier. When she returned in the pre-dawn hours of the morning, intoxicated, Betsey managed to tack the train ticket to Tim's bedroom door with a nail using the bottom of her shoe as a hammer. Letting out a laugh, she stumbled into her room and fell into bed.

Perking up from the sounds outside the door, Tim said with

fatigue, peering from beneath the blankets on his bed, "Why don't you just leave me alone, Mama."

We all came here together from Green Creek. But I decided that losing my sanity, and being something I'm not, aren't a part of my life. I find peace where I can. Zeke's face and voice suddenly emerged from the small round cloudy mirror on the wall.

Merely an hour later, and without a word, Tim quietly packed the laundry bag with all he owned, including his butler's uniform used at the Benson home and the cigar box. The cold water in the white enamel washbasin caused him to shiver as he freshened his body with lye soap in anticipation of a long train ride. He smiled sadly and sighed with relief while inspecting the room that at one point housed his brothers.

"I'll never come back. That's a promise."

Taking his only coat from the wall hook, he unlocked the door and turned the bedroom doorknob slowly until it made a small clicking noise. He opened it just far enough to release his body and the sack of possessions. He paused when Betsey's bed creaked briefly, then stopped. The stench of alcohol seeped into the hall from beneath her door and her rhythmic snoring continued.

The train ticket to Abingdon attached to the bedroom door received only slight notice. Tim walked delicately to the living room, then stopped to turn back. He looked down the short hallway, the source of scuffles, pain, and sadness, while tears flooded his eyes. It was not the train ticket prominently displayed on the door that paralyzed his feet but the sound from Betsey's room growing louder. He pressed his hands to his ears and dropped to his knees.

"I need this pain to stop," he whispered in anguish.

As he lifted his head, struggling to raise his writhing body, the train ticket on the door faded from his sight.

Tim patted his breast pocket and pulled out the letter from the Bensons' Canadian guests—*Vous trouverez ci-joint 50 dollars et un billet de train pour Renfrew, Ontario, Canada. Venez rejoindre notre équipe. Envoyez un télégramme à l'adresse ci-dessous pour confirmer. Signé Mme Janvier*—then replaced it inside his coat with the telegram giving instructions for his arrival.

Turning toward the front door once again, he threw the bag over his shoulder and made his way to the station to board a train to Canada.

CHAPTER 17

THE IDENTITY (1926)

The train's motion rocked him. Like a baby, Tim dozed off. During the deepest sleeps, fists landed blows to his body. Betsey's face grimaced. In the light moments of sleep, sounds of men's voices teasing and mocking, and then unexpectedly the sun revealed a lifeless body on the ground. Its face smashed. One eyeball hanging from the socket. Blood mixed with dirt to make a thick red soup surrounding torn clothes.

"Ticket," the conductor said loudly.

Tim startled upward in the seat. "What?"

"Your ticket. Either hand me your ticket or jump off a moving train."

Tim pulled the ticket from his shirt pocket. His hands shook as he passed the paper to the conductor. The conductor's eyes widened, carefully reading each word, then he pulled the pen from his hat and made some marks.

"Renfrew, Ontario. Ontario is a long way from Morriston, Alabama. What takes you there?"

"Why?" Tim grabbed the ticket and shoved it in his pocket.

"Nervous folks like you are probably running from trouble," he said, then noticed the anger welling up in the brown-and-green speckled eyes of the young man with curly hair and olive skin.

Tim turned his face to the window.

"The conductor was just making conversation, Tim," said Kelvin.

Tim's head rotated toward the Pullman porter who stood behind the conductor.

"I didn't tell you my name. Who are you?" His chest heaved up and down and his hands grabbed the arms of the bench so tightly his knuckles protruded beneath the skin.

"Kelvin. Saw your name on the ticket. I'll let you be."

Tim turned back toward the window, where the world rushed by. Trees blurred. Smoke from the train obscured his view of nature. Finally, he settled into his seat, wrapping his chest and neck with the coat to say cozy. He used the laundry bag of personal items for a pillow. And, once again, sleep consumed the world inside the train.

Three days blurred from night dreams and daydreams. Loneliness did not factor in due to phantom visits from the welcome, like Kate and Mr. Larry, and the unwelcome, like Betsey and Master Hatch. New passengers sitting next to Tim interjected moments of reality.

"Boy, you have a transfer here. End of the line. Wake up," the conductor said, shaking Tim's shoulder.

Tim's head bobbed.

"Mama, stop. I'm waking up."

"I'm not your mama. Take your ticket out and make your transfer. You're the only one left on this train."

Tim cowered in his seat. Eyes darting. "Where am I?"

"I got him," Kelvin said. "Tim, you're on a train, remember? You're riding to Renfrew, Ontario. This is the Chicago Union

Station where you transfer to the train into Canada. Here. Let me help you."

"Right, I was in a deep sleep and forgot. I'm OK. Thanks, Kelvin."

"No problem. Grab your bag. I'll walk with you."

Rows of passenger cars lined the expansive concrete tunnel. Tim grabbed his bag and followed Kelvin past the empty seats and onto the platform. Steam, heat, and coal dust filled the tunnel. Locomotives roared in the background, mixing with elevated voices and the pattering of scurrying feet.

"Hurry, Tim, stay with me, your train leaves soon. By the way, what's your last name?"

"Brisco."

"Yes. That's what I remembered from your ticket. Any relation to Dub Brisco?"

"Why?"

Tim stopped. Kelvin, unaware, proceeded at a fast pace. Tim looked around, reading the platform signs. He looked at his ticket and the transfer information, then stopped another passing porter to confirm the location of the Canadian National to Renfrew. By that time, Kelvin noticed Tim's reluctance.

Approaching, Kelvin said, "You can trust me. Just making conversation again. Morriston's a small place."

"My name is simply Tim, and you're simply the Pullman porter. You should be helping the folks with their bags. I can't afford to give you a tip. I got this. Point the way and I'll go."

"'Simply' helping, man. That's all. Sometimes, we all need a little help," he said, patting Tim on the back. "Your train is right here. Good luck on whatever you're heading to. Lots of our folks have been moving to Canada for one reason or another. A little too cold in that region for me. I hope you brought a heavier coat or money to buy one." Kelvin chuckled and tipped his hat.

Tim nodded and said, "I'm set."

"OK. I'll take my leave here and go back to my train. Be careful, Simply Tim."

Tim turned around and took the last step toward the new life he sought.

CHAPTER 18

THE DESTINATION
(1926–1927)

Finding a seat in a near-empty and cold car on the Canadian National, Tim placed his ticket in a metal clip above the bench as Kelvin had instructed. Once again, he pulled the coat tightly around his body but could not alleviate the sting of the cooler northern weather penetrating his bones. Eyeing the corner fold of a gray wool military blanket on the ledge above the seat, he yanked it down and fully enclosed himself in a cocoon and laid his head on the laundry bag. All anyone could see were eyes and a small lock of hair protruding from a peep hole. The warmth engulfed his body, causing the muscles in his arms and back to finally relax while he emitted a slow sigh of satisfaction for the upcoming day-and-a-half ride to his destination.

    He'd never experienced such restful bouts of sleep. Through the fog of a twilight slumber, the conductor yelled "Renfrew, Ontario!" From the blanket cocoon he emerged looking clear eyed, rested, and carefree as a butterfly. The telegram from the new employers contained all the information he needed.

With some command of the French language, he sought directions to the home and soon found himself striding up a gravel sidewalk to a large domicile built of limestone—the residence of the Janviers, a prominent textile family. The surrounding vegetation indicated a different climate from Morriston.

A footman answered the door and immediately greeted Tim by name and title—"butler." A fireplace in nearly every room on the first floor infused warmth throughout. With the family away in Vancouver, the other servants trained Tim and prepared him for service upon their return.

Staff stayed in quarters beneath the house. The four male staff—a chauffeur, groundsman, footman, and butler—stayed in two shared rooms. The three female staff—a cook, an upstairs maid, and a downstairs maid—shared another room.

Compared to Betsey's home, the furniture and other accommodations for Mme Janvier's workers improved Tim's lifestyle. A properly sized wool butler's uniform, including shoes, socks, and gloves, lay on the bed assigned to Tim. In preparation for his duties, Tim spent time with each staff person, learning the running of the house and the specific responsibilities for the wine cellar, inventory of the china, silver and crystal, and general oversight of the workers.

Tim settled into the butler position, applying what he learned from Mr. Larry and Mr. David. Approximately the size of Morriston and much like working for the Bensons, his life became simple and routine in Renfrew.

***

Tim did not mind the extreme cold during the winter months, preferring the snow over the hot stifling summers of Alabama.

The vast weather changes matched his moods, and the culture did not offer much more than nature and solitude. As a result, he neither ventured far from the mansion nor fostered a personal relationship with the other servants.

"Tim, you've been here at least a couple of months now and I still don't know much about you," Miss Jane, the cook, said while studiously stirring a pot of beef stew. "I'll be honest. I'm beginning to wonder if you're hiding something or maybe escaping something."

"I don't have much to say," Tim said, shrugging.

"Fair enough. I guess the most important thing is that Mme Janvier likes you. She told me you made a good impression during their visit to the States. They're happy you came. I bet you didn't know how small this town is."

"It didn't matter."

"Why don't you go outside and explore the stores and people? I haven't even seen you leave this yard since you came here in late summer."

"I saw the whole town when I first arrived. That was enough."

"But you haven't seen Montreal, Québec, and Ottawa, Ontario. They are a short ride eastward. If you take time off, there are plenty of Negroes living and working in the cities. Lots of jazz music in Montreal too, if you're into that."

"OK" was all he said.

With the Christmas bonus from Mme Janvier, he walked to the secondhand store to shop for a heavy wool coat, gloves, and hat. While in the store, he also bought a well-tailored double-breasted lounge suit with broad shoulders, a matching vest, high-waisted trousers, a white shirt, and wing-tip shoes. The Christmas festivities, New Year's celebration, and consistent encouragement from Miss Jane provided a new perspective on life.

Two weeks later, on his first day off in the new year, he applied pomade to slick back his hair, removing any evidence of the curls, put on the new clothes, and boarded the Canadian National for a twenty-four-hour excursion.

"Sir, your ticket please. Thank you. Headed to Montreal, huh?" the conductor asked.

"Yes," Tim said. "Can you recommend a place to enjoy some jazz music?"

"Jazz?" the conductor said with raised eyebrows and shaking his head.

"Yes. Is there a problem?"

"No problem, sir. Not many people of your stature ask for that type of recommendation."

Tim's brown-and-green-speckled eyes widened.

"No offense, sir," the conductor said, stuttering. "A well-dressed businessman such as yourself, well, I expected you to ask for a different recommendation like fine dining and dancing or a gentleman's club. But I'm happy to oblige. I highly recommend Stacey's Corner. A porter friend quit the rails and opened the joint last year. It's classy and some of the top artists from the United States perform there too. It's real popular. If you need a place to stay, Stacey has rooms on the second floor and the Hotel Elliot is next door too."

"Thank you." Tim nodded.

Businessman? Me? he thought. He turned to look out the window. A man much paler than when he lived in Alabama stared back at him. The flecks of green in his eyes somehow dominated the more subtle brown. The shiny pin-straight hair parted on the side visually altered his appearance.

He stepped off the train. Men tipped their hats or nodded. Women gave a smile bordering on flirtatious, looking at him from head to toe. "I'm not invisible! I'm one of them now," he said under his breath.

You think you're better than the rest of us with your proper talk. Betsey's voice exploded in his head. His gloved fists balled up, remembering his own words to her while seeing his reflection rapidly flash across multiple windows as he walked past the station's facade. *Look at me! I'm not Tuttle's son. Look at my skin. I'm not brown. Look at my hair. It's not frizzy or kinky. Look at my eyes. They have specks of brown and green. I look whiter than you. But in this country, I'm stuck because I'm your son. Now, Mother dear, I'm going far away where none of this matters. I'm not the son of a brown indentured servant or a stinking drunk.*

Snowflakes landed on his face, reminiscent of the droplets of Betsey's spit. Fervently wiping the moisture away, he declared loudly, "I am better than you, Mama."

He pulled his shoulders firmly back, focusing on the world in front of him instead of the sidewalk and people's feet. With directions to Stacey's Corner from the conductor, he arrived at the show bar located on the corner of de la Montagne and Craig Street, took a seat at a small table, and ordered a generous pour of Scotch.

People of all colors filled Stacey's Corner, disregarding their color differences. Failure to embrace the latest clothing fashions—like flapper dresses and cloche hats for women and wingtip shoes and fedoras for men—drew looks of disapproval.

For Tim, intoxication from the instruments' sounds in the club conjured one of the few pleasant memories of sitting at the tavern in Low Orchard, swaying to the rhythm of a jazz trio. Women gazed at him most of the night, offering many unsolicited introductions.

At sunup, he caught the first train back to Renfrew.

***

Throughout the summer, he repeated the same trip to Montreal. Soon, the musicians and patrons at Stacey's Corner all knew Tim.

On an unusually hot night, patrons overflowed the bar, and the mingling scents of alcohol and perfume intoxicated the atmosphere as a new artist, Louis Armstrong, drew a large crowd with his unique style of playing the cornet and trumpet. Tim sat at his usual table, alone. Stacey, the bar owner, reserved the table each Saturday for Tim, with one extra chair, which remained empty.

After he sat through two jazz sets, a drunken, pencil-shaped, petite woman with a stylish bobbed haircut, plain faced yet fashionably dressed in flapper-girl attire, approached the empty chair, sporting a cigarillo held between her thumb and pointer. The pinky finger stood at attention, wrapped in a diamond-studded band.

"This Louis Armstrong is the best! What a crazy night! Big crowd and nowhere to sit, huh? My name is Marguerite Bouchard. Do you mind?" she said as she eased herself into the empty chair at Tim's table.

Courteously, he stood up.

"Sure, sit down, please," he said, wiping sweat from his forehead with a handkerchief and taking his own seat.

"Don't bother telling me your name. Everyone knows you. You don't have the air of a Canadian. I've only been here barely a year myself. I'm from Paris. I can tell you are from the States."

"France? I've always wanted to live in France," he said, leaning in to hear the young woman's every word.

Over the remainder of the evening until closing at four in the morning, Louis Armstrong provided the soundtrack to Marguerite's tales of life in France. Tim learned she was from a wealthy family in the lumber business, had a sister one year younger, and a brother two years older. Her father moved the family to Montreal to expand the business. In return, Tim offered little about his past, or present.

Between Tim's reclusive life and Marguerite's efforts to learn all she could as a new resident of Montreal, their acquaintance quickly became amicable. In short order, he negotiated with Mme Janvier to have both Sundays and Mondays off every week instead of just Sundays. The footman was happy to cover for him and receive the extra wages. Now when he spent two days in Montreal, each visit started with a greeting from Marguerite, who anticipated his arrival by rail.

***

In the fall, she expressed a desire to advance their relationship.

"I have a request of you," Marguerite said upon meeting him at the station.

"And what is that, my friend," Tim replied.

"Instead of our usual walk to breakfast and exploring the city, I told my family that I'm bringing someone to meet them."

"What? I'm not prepared or dressed appropriately. Why?"

"You look fine. Please. They're expecting you, and if you don't meet them, then I can't see you again. I'll be humiliated."

He glimpsed himself in the train station window. Every hair lay in place, shoes shined, shirt starched, and suit clean. He relinquished.

The taxicab drove them to a home much larger and grander than anything in Morriston, Talladega, or Renfrew. She jumped from the car immediately upon the driver opening the door.

"Come!" she said, beckoning with her hand.

He slid from the car seat and reluctantly approached Marguerite, following her up the stairs of a twenty-thousand-square-foot home made of white stone, flanked with eight towering ornate marble columns spanning three floors. The butler anticipated their arrival, holding open the tall front door decorated with swirled wrought-iron configurations protecting intricately designed stained glass.

"Where's the family?" she said excitedly to the man dressed in a uniform very similar to Tim's for his job in Renfrew.

"In the breakfast room, ma'am," he said dryly.

"Let's go, Tim. I must warn you my father will say little to nothing, my mother will ask a million questions, my sister will expect you to be mesmerized by her because she is truly stunningly beautiful, and my brother will finish eating and go about his business."

Because he was busily looking around at the ornate architecture, Marguerite's recitation of the family dynamics did not capture his attention. He marveled at the various marble, tile, and parquet flooring, and the frescoes and intricate moldings lining the ceiling throughout. The furniture brought to life pictures of the Palace of Versailles, which he'd studied in his quest to learn about France.

Finishing the diatribe about her family, the couple arrived in a room where Betsey's entire home in Morriston could fit. Flowers sat on every table, creating a rose aerosol throughout. The patio windows welcomed sunlight throughout the entire morning, accenting the hand-painted designs of the tile floor. A server stood in the corner, anticipating every need of each family member. The father and mother flanked each end of the table, and the brother sat facing Tim with an inconsequential look. The sister remained hidden by the height of a tall mahogany chair.

"Everyone, this is Tim, the man I mentioned whom I'm officially declaring my boyfriend."

Tim emitted a slight nervous chuckle at the announcement. He scanned each person at the table while taking in the vastness of the room. Finally, the sister turned in her chair to inspect Marguerite's beau. The young lady let out a loud giggle. A memorable voice from Upper Orchard followed, igniting a reverberation in his temples. His mind shot back to his first meeting with his beloved Kate years prior. Willingly repeated, the eerily familiar dialogue flowed without effort.

"Who are you again?" she said.

Tim instinctively rubbed his hands on his pants and nodded his head to release the words caught in his throat.

"Who are you?" she asked again.

"Tim, ma'am."

"That's what I thought. My name is Cateline, but call me Cate. I've seen you at Stacey's Corner several times. You're quite popular. My sister and I spied on you many times from a dark corner next to the bar. I've been writing about you in my diary. Watching you has been amusing since the beginning of the year. But who are you? Where are you from?"

He blinked several times. His temples throbbed and his mind raced. *Her words. Her voice,* he thought.

"Like I said, you've been part of the club scene for a long time. Unlike my sister, I did not dare be so forward to venture and see the world from your vantage point. It's not ladylike. One day you must tell me what fascinates you and keeps you coming back to the jazz world here."

His eyes took in an olive-skinned girl with long, flowing black curly hair. The room transformed to the yard outside the parlor window where he and Kate Russo met beneath the far-reaching branches and expansive trunk of the walnut tree.

"Kate?" Tim said.

"Yes?" Cate said.

Marguerite said, "Are you OK, Tim? You're flushed."

"Sorry. I'm fine. You're sure we haven't met before?" Tim asked, looking at Cate Bouchard.

She stared at him quizzically. She looked just like Kate Russo.

Clearing his throat and wiping his mouth with a starched linen napkin, the father said, "Marguerite, please mind yourself. You don't declare a man your 'boyfriend' in that way. As Cate said, you have not exemplified very ladylike manners."

"Oh, Father," Mrs. Bouchard said. "Marguerite has never had a boyfriend, so we can pardon her exuberance. She's not like our Cate who must shoo away the young men."

"Not true!" Marguerite said.

The brother shook his head. "Can I be excused? I'm not ready for this calamity."

"Yes," Mr. Bouchard said.

"Oh, and I'm Alexandre, by the way. Nice meeting you." The brother stood, stretching more than six feet tall with broad shoulders and a stern, chiseled face, shook Tim's hand with an excessively firm grip, and walked out of the room.

"Have a seat," the mother said, motioning to a chair next to Cate. "I understand you just arrived in Montreal. Please have some breakfast and we can chat."

"So you've now met the family, tell us about yourself. You have an unusual accent," Mr. Bouchard said.

"Father, where are your manners? Tim, I insist. Please sit. Addy, attend to our guest first," Mrs. Bouchard commanded the server.

Tim hesitated, then pulled out the chair and focused on the embroidery in the seat upholstery. When he looked up, the room transformed into Betsey's kitchen. The familiarity of the small table put Tim at ease. In front of him sat the plate. A fork lay to the left, the knife and spoon to the right. The napkin folded into a diamond shape, then set to the left of the fork. All lined up as straight as a ruler, just as Tim had performed that day when he was eight years old and all the years after at the Benson's home.

The server brought freshly baked breakfast ham sliced into thin pieces and arranged from smallest to largest on a porcelain serving dish. The attendant promptly returned with a white-cloth-covered basket filled with warm bread and a bowl of scrambled eggs. Tim's glass at the top right of the plate was filled with water from a crystal pitcher by the server.

That's what it feels like, he thought.

Cate fondled her hair, smiled at Tim, and slightly rolled her eyes in her sister's direction.

Tim smiled in return.

After the mother oversaw the breakfast service details, she immediately reverted to the father's question. Tim quickly crafted a story based on stories he'd heard while serving upper-class people at the Janviers' home.

He was born an only child in Alabama but was orphaned when his parents died from illnesses when he was ten years old. His grandparents, now deceased, raised him. He attended a couple of years at a small college in Alabama, no place like a renowned Ivy League, and decided to sell the property he inherited. In a class at the college called The New Era, the professor discussed Renfrew when teaching the shift in North America because of its growing lumber and textile businesses. He was pursuing the dream of starting his own business and aspired to own a grand hotel, so he was learning about hospitality and culinary arts. He regularly visited Montreal to learn about the entertainment business and might open a restaurant, even expand to France.

"Well, what a story and how ambitious that you can leave the States and simply follow your dream. That's how wealth starts. What do you know of your European heritage? What is your lineage? Who are your people?" Mr. Bouchard asked.

"I'm sorry, sir, my parents died so early in my life. My grandparents didn't tell me much and died only a few years later."

"By your looks, I would venture to guess your people are from the Mediterranean, maybe even France—"

"Well, it doesn't much matter. And at some point, you can effortlessly find your family in Europe," Mrs. Bouchard said. "We love your ambition. I must say you're a handsome young man. I love those green eyes of yours."

Cate giggled. Marguerite, sitting opposite her sister, pouted when she noticed that Cate's eyes never left Tim and his focus always returned to Cate's hands delicately folded in front of her plate.

Each night at bedtime thereafter, Kate Russo's voice and looks infiltrated his sleep and spurred dreams of Upper Orchard.

Throughout the fall and into the winter months, Tim and Marguerite spent each week on his days off planning a restaurant and dreaming of France. The young lady never invited him back to her home. Cate never returned to the jazz club with her sister. And Tim never inquired about the family.

CHAPTER 19

SUCCESS (1927)

To start the coal machine miner training, Jimmy Tappers placed Dub in one of the underground drift mines.

The promotion further distanced him from the good graces of his Tarboro neighbors. They saw the change in the Briscos' standard of living and favoritism with the Tapperses. Within the first year of his promotion, he bought his house outright. With the additional income came a used black pickup truck and other household pleasures. Driving to work, his head faced forward, passing coworkers using only their feet for transportation. Some gave Dub brief nods or watched the truck amble down the street; others ignored his air of superiority.

The workdays at Tappers and friction with the Tarboro community continued in this fashion over the first year after the promotion.

He took on an additional job for extra money to build out his property. Handwritten notes delivered to the mailboxes of upscale neighborhood homes advertised his curbside hauling service for a nominal fee. Then, early Saturday morning each week, he drove the pickup truck to the wealthy side of Abingdon. Cruising by the front of each home from time to time revealed furniture, tools, or appliances deposited outside for him to dispose of or salvage. He used the better items in his own home or resold them to Tarboro residents. The money from the arduous work became more evident over the years, as he had the best-looking home in Tarboro.

"The furniture you've been bringing home has made this house look better than any I've ever seen," Mae said. "How does it compare to Kelvin's house back in Morriston? Ours is much better than the teacher's house here in Tarboro. I think this house is ready to show off."

Looking up from a newspaper, Dub said, "What you've done to the house is wonderful. I can't tell you how it compares to Kelvin's. Though Kelvin made it a little better than the way Miss Clara left it."

"What? Ours is as ornate as Miss Clara's in Morriston and now you're telling me Kelvin's wife made Miss Clara's home even better? Why didn't you tell me? What exactly is better at Kelvin's house? I must learn proper decorating. And I never see the grand homes that you visit on Saturdays, so I can only imagine. I rely on you to tell me these things."

"Really? Damn it, I do the best I can. Is it ever enough? Am I not doing enough? I work two jobs. I bring all the fine items for free. You say you want more. But tell me how to achieve that."

Mae said, "One thing you can do is take me with you occasionally on Saturdays when you go to find treasures. Maybe I can look inside some of the windows while sitting in the truck."

"Seriously? If it's that important to you, just invite a lady from the church over who cooks or cleans the wealthy folks' homes. She can tell you where you are lacking in the niceties in here. I don't want you riding around in my truck gawking at the rich people's houses."

"I don't talk to the women who do domestic work anymore," she replied. "I overheard a woman at church say you have prestige in Tarboro because you have the best coal mining job of all the Negroes at Tappers. Well, either way, I'm inviting Mrs. Kirkland, the pastor's wife, over. I plan to entertain her in the parlor by the warm stove. I'll freshly starch the white cotton napkins to lay on our laps as we talk about the church, etiquette, and raising children. I'll pick bouquets of fresh flowers from the yard to accent the rooms. Then, she can tell all of Tarboro we have the finest home, despite the six children."

Turning away to focus on shining the wood-and-marble top of the china cabinet, Mae said, "While the pastor's wife is here, I trust the children will behave and play outside. Can you supervise them to make sure each one is doing outside chores or constructive play during that time?"

Bernie, Amaya, and Genese helped with Mae's household responsibilities, including cooking, sewing, washing, cleaning, and ironing, and Matthew and Calvin apprenticed beside Dub, doing carpentry, plumbing, gardening, hauling, and hunting. The children were not allowed to step foot outside if they were not in fresh clean clothes or did not have every hair in place. She carefully guarded who the children befriended in Tarboro. If the other child did not live in a home much like the Briscos', then they were not a suitable friend.

"Dub, I wish you had more friends we could invite over too. Why don't you talk to the lovely man that owns the store. Mr. Johnson? I think he's a widow and his children are so well mannered. From what I can see, it seems to me Mr. Johnson does quite well financially and has one of the older church ladies clean his home."

Dub said nothing more and returned to reading the newspaper.

CHAPTER 20

THE ROOM (1927–1928)

By the end of the year, Tim and Marguerite had toured all the important sights, clubs, and restaurants money could buy in Montreal. Ultimately, the Hotel Elliot became their weekend home.

Each Sunday, upon Tim's arrival, they frequented a restaurant to eat breakfast, then checked into a corner room.

Room 205 allowed a view of the sidewalk to see guests arriving or leaving Stacey's Corner from the north. The west side gave a view of the city park benches frequented by residents taking strolls and nannies pushing prams.

The tapestry wallpaper in a muted gold pattern of overlaid grapevines created a comfortable feeling of home. A single frosted-glass bowl chandelier hung from the ceiling, supplementing the natural light from windows covered with gold silk curtains and fringed valances. A vanity and writing desk completed the room but remained unused except to hold jewelry and playing cards. A fireplace and rug added more warmth for bare feet.

The couple lazed most of the afternoon, lounging in two stuffed living room chairs, with their clothes parked in the armoire or dresser. They always found their way to a four-poster wood bed covered with a heavy white wool fringed blanket.

By December, they were spending the cold days after lunch huddled in bed, making plans or sharing the events of the previous week. Tim became masterful at spinning an alternative life in Renfrew and discouraging Marguerite from desiring to visit.

Later in the day, Marguerite went home for formal dinners with the family as required by Mrs. Bouchard. Afterward she changed clothes for evening jazz entertainment with Tim. At the club's closing, Tim hailed a cab for Marguerite's return home.

Some evenings he arranged for other female guests to meet in his room or for a game of cards with club musicians. On Monday, the pair repeated the schedule, the only difference being Tim took the last train to Renfrew in the evening.

***

Delivering news of her pregnancy to Tim in late January, Marguerite said, "What do we do? I can't be shamed in this community."

"Of course," he said. From the north window a sliver of light came through the drapes and a vision of the window frame of Mr. Thomas's office reflected on the curtains. Tim replayed their conversation in his mind.

I'm so sorry. Son, you can't do anything about it now. Under normal circumstances, you should take care of that responsibility. But an Upper Orchard white girl? They will deal with it for you, so, you can't let this deprive you of the life you could have otherwise. The best thing to do is forget her, forget the baby, go to Talladega, and move on.

But those people in Upper Orchard are taking my child and Kate from me. You're telling me I have no voice or choice? I'm tired of being told to stay invisible when it comes to dealing with those people. Is there nothing I can control?

Look, Tim, those people are doing what's best for you and that girl. With some things in this world you have no choice. But you do have control over whether you become successful in your life, despite the circumstances. You're a smart young man. Now is the time to use those smarts. Trust me, that girl will move on. Especially if they see a brown baby come out of her. . . . Son, the truth is you must prepare to move on without her.

"Tim. Do you understand?" Marguerite said.

"Yes, I understand. I will stop my trips here and stay in Renfrew, and you can do what you and your family must. I know how this works."

"What do you mean 'stay in Renfrew' and you 'know how this works'? Leave me in this condition? How dare you! I thought you were an honorable man. You must marry me and look after me and this child!"

"What? I didn't think you would want to marry someone like me. Plus, I don't come from your social circles. Don't your parents want you to marry someone rich and highly educated like them? And wouldn't we have to leave Canada to avoid any skepticism?"

"What are you talking about?" She stared at Tim curiously. "It will be OK if we marry, and we must. We'll simply tell people that the baby was born a little early. Money shouldn't be a problem. You have the money from the inherited property you sold. Right? We can start off with that, and my father will help too, I'm sure. And then we open our restaurant."

Within a month Marguerite announced her pregnancy to the Bouchards. Already disconnected from family in Morriston and with nothing to lose, Tim gave two weeks' notice to Mme Janvier with the news that he'd secured new employment in music and moved to Montreal.

The couple had a quiet wedding ceremony on the Bouchards'

property with only immediate family present. The father gave the newlyweds enough money to start a restaurant, saying it was a "dowry" of sorts, and a residence on the estate until the birth of the baby. The pair settled into a one-story, two-bedroom and two-bathroom bungalow amid a dense manicured French garden in the back, secluded from the mansion.

Marguerite commanded the fully stocked kitchen and domestic chores, while Tim mimicked the protocols and etiquette of a wealthy man. With access to the Bouchards' money, during the day Tim traversed into town to frequent jazz clubs while feigning plans to open a restaurant. And well into the summertime, he gambled and drank while masking his loneliness and lack of desire for work.

Other times, he walked the grounds of the estate, pausing to watch Cate lounging by the pool. The swimsuit accentuated the curves of her body, unlike Marguerite's pencil-thin frame before pregnancy. The oil Cate sensually spread across her legs and chest caused a rise in Tim's desire. Cate's eyes locked with his and she positioned her arms above her head, arching her back to enlarge and expose her cleavage, but he dared not approach. Resigned to his marital status, he returned to the guesthouse.

Two nights later, on a clear, warm late-July evening, with the moon in full view, Tim bid Marguerite farewell to have an after-dinner drink at Stacey's Corner. Cate, from her bedroom window, saw him dressed in a tan summer suit with loose high-waisted pants, two-toned shoes, a silk tie, and a pocket handkerchief. Pomade kept every hair straight and in place with a clean part on the side.

Cate turned to the wardrobe and grabbed a flowy lime-colored summer dress, white T-strap heels, and three long strands of pearl necklaces and wound her hair tight in a knot at the base of her neck, replicating a bobbed style. Spray from a crystal perfume bottle emitted a cloud of sweet musk that enveloped her body. She nodded with satisfaction to the woman she saw in the vanity mirror.

Bidding her family farewell in the parlor, she hopped in the Bouchards' chauffeured car and barked orders to take her to Stacey's Corner. Upon arrival, the driver opened the car door for his passenger. Notes from "Rhapsody in Blue" floated from the club, welcoming every guest.

"I will hail a cab home," Cate said, exiting the car. "And by the way, you dropped me off at Gisele's home to play bridge."

Seated in a dark shadow of the bar, Tim felt a tap on the shoulder. He looked up and her smile captured his attention.

"Hello."

Her voice transformed the room to the gardeners' storage shed at the back of Kate Russo's estate. Cate Bouchard's eyes mirrored that first night he and Kate Russo became intimate and the many nights afterward. He took her hand and eased her into his lap. She did not resist the delicate kiss he placed on her lips and the caress around her buttocks.

"My Kate. I knew you would return."

The pair spent the evening cuddling and fondling each other between shots of whiskey and dancing the slow drag, bumping, and grinding. Patrons in the jazz club had an unspoken code to disregard improper behavior, although many witnessed Tim's provocative dancing and efforts to seduce his wife's sister.

At the end of the evening, with Marguerite asleep, Tim removed his shoes and tiptoed into the guesthouse. Retrieving the cigar box from the back of his armoire, where it was hidden behind a stack of new shoes, he retreated to the library to read the letters from Kate and look at the pencil drawing of the baby.

Afterward, Tim's world reverted to voyeuristic excursions reminiscent of Upper Orchard. Once the sun set and the house lights lit the grounds, he commenced traversing the estate, peering inside to find Cate. She caught glimpses of Tim lurking. In rooms where she gathered with family, she positioned herself within view of a window, much like on a stage, and assured that her behavior was sensually animated without provoking questions from others.

The excursion climaxed beneath her window, where he waited among the shrubbery, hoping to catch a peek. While preparing for bed, she removed her clothes, clutched her breasts, and then raised her arms to slip into a thin white cotton nightgown. A deep throaty laugh emerged as she watched Tim's entire body writhing with pleasure. She doled out the exhibition three times over the following two weeks, priming him for their next meeting.

As usual, on an early-September morning after finishing the breakfast Marguerite prepared, Tim departed the guesthouse. He walked to the front of the estate to exit the gate onto the main street when a voice called out from a distance, "Mr. Brisco!"

The chauffeur turned in a circle, assuring no other family members lingered within view. He ran to Tim.

"This is for you." He slyly pushed a small envelope into Tim's hands and jogged away, returning to wipe down the car in the driveway as if nothing had taken place.

Tim stopped a block away from the mansion to read the message.

The unsigned note said, *Meet me at twelve noon in room 205 of the Hotel Elliot.* "Who told her about 205?" Tim muttered out loud.

Thereafter, Tim and Cate met each afternoon during the week, in the same room, then returned home to family. Later, they reconvened after family dinner at a jazz club or dance hall until midnight, much like Tim had done with Marguerite during their courtship.

In the meantime, Marguerite's belly grew slowly during the pregnancy. Weeks before the due date, her sense of loneliness and Tim's abandonment became intolerable.

"Tim, come feel the baby move," Marguerite said, placing

his hand on her belly when he returned to the guesthouse for dinner.

"That is amazing," he said, putting his hat on the foyer table. "Why don't you go to bed and rest. You're due soon. Right?"

"Yes, but are you joining me?"

"Maybe later. I have some reading to do."

"Other than feeling the baby move, you haven't been intimate with me since the month we were married."

"You're pregnant. I don't want to hurt the baby."

"Are you sure that is all?"

"Yes, please go to bed. I will tuck you in."

As soon as he saw her eyes close, he removed his shoes and quietly walked to the armoire to retrieve the cigar box. Marguerite peered into the library, observing tears rising in Tim's eyes as he held his head.

The next morning after breakfast, as usual, he departed the guesthouse to walk into town. Despite being in the final weeks of pregnancy, Marguerite had sufficient stamina to keep pace a block behind him. She recognized the route to Stacey's Corner, but when he passed the entrance, confusion and curiosity settled in with the belief that maybe he had found a nearby restaurant to buy. When he entered the lobby of Hotel Elliot next door, nausea welled up inside her belly.

From the city park across the street, she sat on a bench far enough away to watch the entrance. Soon, the light turned on in room 205. Less than five minutes later, Cate entered the lobby. She watched the shadows of a woman and a man frolic behind the drapes periodically.

Marguerite rose from the bench for an agonizing walk home, occasionally stopping to absorb periodic labor pains. At the guesthouse, without hesitation, she opened the armoire to search for the cigar box and papers Tim had read the night before. Despite the volatile episodes of contractions, she visited the mansion to share the discovery with her parents, including the story of Kate Russo, the truth about Tim, and the relationship with Cate.

Four hours later, Tim and Cate left the hotel moments apart and entered the jazz club. When Cate arrived home for family dinner, the butler escorted her to the parlor, where Mr. and Mrs. Bouchard and Alexandre had prepared for her return with a plan. By the time Tim arrived at the guesthouse for dinner and opened the door, Marguerite sat in the living room, his cigar box cradled in her lap and Kate Russo's letters and pencil drawings of a baby lying at her feet.

"You're a colored man. You're colored! The fetus I'm carrying is colored! You're screwing my sister too? How could you do this? On top of it, you never loved me. You loved this white girl Kate in these letters, whoever she is. Why are you here destroying my family? Go back to her family and your child with her! But I guess she doesn't want you either."

"I can't go back. She's dead. And I don't know where the little girl is and—"

A fist banged multiple times on the door. Marguerite and Tim froze.

Tim closed his eyes, and when he opened them, the one-room wood-frame home Tuttle built on Green Creek plantation opened around him. The scene played out and the words of Hatch Brisco channeled through the Bouchards.

Muffled sounds of angry arguing voices came from the outside.

"Sounds like Father. I also hear Mother and Alexandre," Marguerite said, tears streaming down her face as she held her contracting belly.

The door shook, but the lock kept it sealed.

"Who is it?" Tim said.

"You know who it is," Mr. Bouchard said. "Open this door."

"We're preparing for bed, Master Hatch."

"Master Hatch? Open this door if you know what's good for you."

"Please, sir, my wife is indisposed," Tim said.

Alexandre said, "Isn't that convenient."

The father banged on the door again. "That's it. You got it coming for you, lowlife."

The butt of a gun broke through the guesthouse window next to the door, and an arm reached through the gaping hole inside to unlock the door. Tim rushed to grab a fireplace poker.

"Get out of here, Master Hatch!" Tim said, swinging the poker in Mr. Bouchard's direction.

Mr. Bouchard aimed the barrel directly at Tim. Everyone in the room paused, and quiet took over.

Marguerite said in a whisper, "Mother. Do something. I think my water broke."

A stream of fluid ran down Marguerite's legs, forming a puddle at her feet.

"Honey, you can't kill him!" Mrs. Bouchard said in a whisper. "Tim, leave this house! Go! We will deal with Marguerite. There's no way we can keep a colored child. It will ruin us. My reputation will never survive it."

"You imposter," Mr. Bouchard growled. "Marguerite told me everything. I didn't like you from the beginning. No past. No pedigree. Violating white women! You're one of those coloreds trying to pass. You defiled my family and home. Take this envelope of money. Grab whatever you brought to Montreal within the next two minutes and get out before I kill you! Trust me, I will do it. No one gives a damn about you. We never want to see your face again."

Tim retrieved the laundry bag from the top of the armoire, grabbed the cigar box and its contents, removed the few clothes from inside the armoire, and stuffed it all in the bag. He exited the house into a dark pathway that morphed into the dense foliage of the road that Tuttle guided his family on northward to Morriston.

Yards down the pathway emerged two broad-shouldered men riding horses branded with the Hatch plantation insignia on the hindquarters. Each man carried a rifle propped across his lap. Other than a brief nod and tip of the hat, the men did not react to Tim, nor did a word pass between the two horsemen.

As he proceeded farther down the pathway, with a signal from one horseman to the other, the men swiftly dismounted and scurried into the bushes, stalking Tim as he neared the gate to the estate. In the darkness of night, with the moon covered by clouds, suddenly, multiple footsteps resounded within the shrubbery and approached Tim, and the silhouettes of the horsemen were revealed: one carrying a bludgeon and the other a rifle. Standing behind shrubs, near the pathway, was the shape of a third man, six feet with broad shoulders and a thin face, ordering the actions of the horsemen.

"This is from Hatch Brisco," a man said ominously. "You thought you'd leave without paying what you owe?"

"Go ahead, hang me from the tree like you did Tuttle, but tell Hatch you hanged his own son," Tim said.

"Who are Tuttle and Hatch? We are here to teach you a lesson for Alexandre," a man said.

"Do it," Alexandre said.

Minutes later, bloodied and bruised, Tim grabbed his bag from the ground. From the street, he looked back through the gates to the estate and the shadow of Cate standing in the driveway.

Tim made his way to Stacey's Corner and tended to his wounds in the men's bathroom. He sat at the bar, swallowing several glasses of Scotch to soothe the pain, occasionally glancing around the room.

"She's not here. I haven't seen her since you were with her," the bartender said. "Be careful, man."

"Too late for that."

He knew the back entrances to the estate and returned to the mansion grounds after the club closed at four a.m. A white marble Roman statue in the flower garden transformed into the angel watching over Kate Russo's grave. Tim sat on a stone bench near the statue.

"Look at me, Kate. I accomplished nothing I promised you. I didn't go to Yale. I didn't even finish Talladega. I'm not rich. I didn't travel any farther than Canada. And our baby is lost."

The angel cried.

Tim stared at Cate's window. No light. No exhibition. Curtains drawn.

His familiarity with the life and place he'd called home for less than a year led him to touch each darkened access to the mansion on the first floor until he peered into the glass french doors of the only room emitting a glow of light.

Marguerite lay in her mother's arms on the couch in the parlor, and the doctor carried an infant swaddled from head to foot. In the corner of the parlor stood the image of Sadie holding the olive-skinned child with big round eyes and rosy cheeks.

"My baby," he said. The baby smiled as it had the night Sadie held the child in the parlor at Kate's coffin.

The doctor placed Marguerite's child in a small cardboard box and softly closed the lid. She screamed and buried her face in Mrs. Bouchard's shoulder. Tim dashed behind the nearest tree, knelt on the ground, and covered his head as it pounded from the screams bouncing off his eardrums. Hearing voices murmuring from the driveway, he looked through the pool of tears to see the doctor's assistant removing the box from the home and carefully placing it in the back of an unmarked black truck. Minutes later, the driver maneuvered down the brick driveway, turning toward the outskirts of town.

The butler draped the ornate curtains across the french

doors, shutting Tim out of any connection to the family. Minutes later, the lights faded to black. Tim sat in darkness.

"What now?" he said, clutching the laundry bag.

Staring into the darkness, he lay supine, compulsively rubbing the outline of the cigar box as tears ran from the corners of his eyes, past his ears, and onto the dirt. After some time, he suddenly rose, slipped the envelope of money from Mr. Bouchard through the mail chute on the front door, and slid away into the black tunnel of thick foliage, emerging outside the estate's gates. He did not stop until arriving at the Montreal train station.

CHAPTER 21

ABINGDON (1928–1929)

As Dub did a regular midnight walk around the perimeter of his yard, a dark figure appeared at the end of the driveway. It approached with a familiar gait. Dub tensed every muscle in his body and stuffed his hands in his pants pockets. Fists clenched.

"Hey, brother," he said.

"Hey, Dub." Tim's grip tightened on the laundry bag containing his only possessions.

"Mama sent that letter over two years ago. Said you were doing some bad stuff."

Tim responded with a nervous chuckle and shrugged. A moment of silence extended as if an entire year were going by. A brief wind blew into his face, filling the void.

"Some stories are never fully told. The rest manifest through our illness and perversities," Tim said.

With a raised voice, Dub said, "Stop the bullshit talk, college boy."

"That's why even you escaped Morriston and didn't look

back, Dub. You couldn't face the past anymore. For me, I couldn't live in the past, and that's why I didn't get off the train here in Abingdon, Illinois, back then. It went all the way to Renfrew, Ontario, Canada."

"What's there? School, I hope?"

"Work. A wife. Some other stuff."

"Where's the wife?"

"Back in Canada. Mistake trying to replace the irreplaceable."

"Humph" was all Dub said.

Silence. Each brother fidgeted. Tim shifted the laundry bag from one side to the other.

Tim said, "Mama?"

"You're too late. Died. Couple of weeks ago. Started drinking more than usual after Zeke got killed in a big mine explosion the week before. She fell off her porch drunk and smashed her head. Quick funeral. Nothing fancy. Nice of you to ask, considering you beat your own mother and you were a drunken embarrassment." Dub rolled his eyes.

"Wait. Zeke. Dead?"

Dub choked up. Tim stood, mouth agape, shaking his head.

"You heard me," Dub replied. "He was doing well. Always mailed Mama money every week. Zeke and I wrote each other short letters once or twice a year, but working in the mines doesn't allow much more." He chuckled, then paused and blinked to hold back his tears while looking at the sky. "Yep. He was Mama's favorite. I sent Zelda some money."

Tim's shoulders curled inward. After taking a deep breath and dropping his head, he said, "What else can I tell you right now?"

The brothers stood in the darkness lit by the moon. Each scanning the night shadows without acknowledging the presence of anything around them, including each other.

Dub finally faced Tim dispassionately, breathed in deeply

and said, "Mae fixed up the shack over there for you when we got Mama's letter."

"Really?" Tim glanced past Dub's shoulder, attempting to see the building through the darkness.

"She'll drop breakfast and dinner at your door."

"OK."

"That's all I got for you. Nothing more. Get your shit together and stay out of my life."

"Right."

The following morning, while they lay cuddled in bed waiting for the children to stir, Dub broke the news to Mae about Tim's late-night arrival.

"It's like Mama and Zeke die, and Tim suddenly resurrects. Great timing."

"Well, most of all, please make sure Tim stays out of sight. What I don't want is people thinking you're like your brother. If he starts drinking like Betsey and starts carousing at bars like he did back home in Morriston, don't go looking for him. The people worth associating with may see you and ostracize us. Then our own children could be rejected because of Tim."

Staring out the window, Dub said, "I don't give Tim's choices any power over me."

***

Months went by and the Briscos continued to be targets in their community, between Mae's efforts to set her family apart from others, Dub's higher position and wage status at Tappers, and Tim's increasing bouts of drunkenness. It went beyond mere gossip and the occasional threatening note or voodoo dolls, and ultimately became something much worse.

"It irks me, Dub, that Tim's got no job and sits in the park ogling at women and kids, and drinks all day," Mae said, eyes squinting while threading the needle of her Singer treadle sewing machine. "And by the way, did Matthew tell you he got into a fight at school? He was put in detention when a group of other boys called him Uncle Tom. I told him the other boys were jealous because we dress better and have a nicer home."

Without taking his eyes off the newspaper, Dub said, "Matthew can take care of himself."

"What about Bernie and Amaya?" Mae asked as she stuffed fabric in the machine, spun the hand wheel, and pumped the pedal. The needle jumped up and down, weaving thread into the garment.

Mae suddenly stopped sewing. "They're not invited to tea parties and birthday parties. But when they told me who hosted the parties, I told them they couldn't go anyway because those families were not up to our standards. At the hair salon, I don't speak to those mothers. They just sit over in the corner and gossip. I'm only making friends with the pastor's wife, teachers, Pullman porters' wives, and the undertaker's wife. These people have invited me for social events too. They're more knowledgeable and make more money."

From behind the newspaper, Dub said, "I'm doing my part."

※※※

During a midnight walk around his property, Dub found himself surrounded by large men with masks. They took turns viciously pushing him until he fell to the ground, where someone gave him a hard kick to the stomach. The air left his lungs. Then came a fist to the head. A piece of wood struck his legs, causing a sharp pain.

Hearing the noises outside, Tim cracked open his door to see multiple shadows in the dark and the sound of his brother's grunts. He watched, eyes growing larger with fear.

"Tuttle's beating on Dub again. I'd better be quiet before Betsey comes swinging at me," Tim whispered.

Each of the attackers picked up a bucket with "TAPPERS" painted in red letters on the side. Coal dust rained down all over Dub where he lay listless on the ground, holding his chest and stomach.

Above him, dripping sweat from the intensity of delivering the blows, a man with a deep familiar voice said, "You're no better than anyone else in Tarboro, especially with a drunk for a brother walking around carrying a cigar box. To the Tappers family, you're just a commodity. Your family will pay the price if you don't start remembering who you are and where you come from. Look at you cower."

Struggling to open his eyes and breathe, Dub caught a glimpse of skin much like his own and faces contorted in anger.

Tim quietly closed the door to the shack, lay down on the cot, and pulled the blanket over his head, while his brother remained beaten on the ground.

Long after the men left, Dub raised himself to his knees, then eventually struggled to stand. "OK, Dub," he whispered to himself with each painful step he took, quietly tiptoeing to the bathroom to clean himself up. "I'd love to kill those bastards. Good thing they didn't hit me in the face," he said, observing the damage in the bathroom mirror. "I can't let Mae see me like this."

CHAPTER 22

UNDERGROUND (1929)

Tim adjusted to his new life in Dub's backyard, learning to maintain an opaque existence. Dub, on the other hand, learned the thrills and perils of operating the new equipment at the mine's surface as a machine miner.

The stock market crash in 1929 and the challenges brought on by the Great Depression did not bypass Tarboro. Occasionally, Dub worked underground, beyond his usual hours on the surface, to make extra money in case he lost his job.

Each excursion underground started similarly. Dub strapped a miner's pick on his back and a small satchel containing food and water around his waist. Walking slightly hunched over down a dark tunnel with dots of bright light ahead, a familiar dampness soaked into his clothes and the cold penetrated his body. He carefully navigated each step into the mine to avoid stumbles or falls.

Before he entered the drift mine, a young boy filled two lamps with oil, igniting each wick. He placed a small lamp on

Dub's hat, and the other in his hand. These would be the only lights to show the way for hundreds of men taking that same path twice a day.

The last thing the boy did was hand the crew supervisor a live caged canary to detect poisonous gases in the mines. The men knew that if the canary fell from its perch, they must evacuate the mine or suffer the same fate from suffocation. There were also risks of cave-ins, fires, and explosions.

Ahead, the tunnel brightened as men congregated. Dub regularly inventoried each face in his crew, men that he worked with each day on the surface or underground who all entrusted their lives to each other. Despite the dim light and layers of black coal dust settling on the skin, he still knew each man by voice and facial shape, and they knew him.

The men of European descent readily talked to him disparagingly, calling him "boy" from time to time. But they watched over each other. One person's slipup could doom them all. Dub fully intended to return to his family each night.

The sound of clanging echoed in his head like gunshots. The picks hit the wall, spraying dust into the air and into their lungs. Striking the wall of rock over and over to extract the coal, his body ached, his hands and arms and muscles fatigued. The men laughed and teased each other to break the tension that built during the grueling work that came as close to the working conditions of slavery than any other job he'd experienced.

"Take a break," said Keenan, the crew supervisor.

Dub sat down and opened the small bag tucked in his satchel that contained the lunch Mae had prepared.

The men squatted in silence along the wall, listening to the melodic splash of water from the mine ceiling dripping onto their hats. In the distance the muffled whirring vibration of drills echoed, and mine cars full of coal rolling along the tracks clacked their way back to the surface.

Keenan's voice rose above the sounds, offering heroic tales

of sexual prowess with his girlfriend the night before. Mucus rattled in his throat from chain smoking and the inhalation of coal dust.

He'd arrived at the mines at the age of ten years old after his father died. Keenan's uncle, one of Jack Tappers's first miners, asked if Jack would give Keenan a job to keep food on the widow's table.

Over the years, Keenan went from being a breaker boy separating coal to crew supervisor. To keep the unions away, he also became the official spy for Jack Tappers.

When Dub first started training underground, Jimmy Tappers assigned Keenan the job to teach Dub mining skills while paying Keenan extra as Dub's protector. At the time of the assignment, Keenan let his feelings be known to Jack when he said, "That boy took a good job from someone who really deserves it."

Keenan, who had a reputation for telling animated stories of his dating life, jumped up. He waved a cigarette in the air while demonstrating how he and his girl with "big boobs" danced sensually.

Dub averted his eyes. He did not care to witness Keenan unbuttoning his shirt to expose a muscular bulging chest almost as large as a female's breasts yet firm, fondling his own nipples to mimic how he grabbed her body, while gyrating his hips.

The caged canary slumped off its perch. Dub pointed. "The bird. Let's go!" he said, and grabbed his lantern.

The explosion shook the entire earth. The men had no time to run. The impact threw Dub to the ground. The tunnel filled with dust and smoke, making it almost impassable. Coal rained like hail as rumbles reverberated in the distance.

A few lanterns withstood the blast of air. Dub grabbed his, still lit and lying next to his leg where he had fallen. His head hurt. He reached for it and realized the light on his hat was out.

He lit it again with his lantern and illuminated men crawling on the ground.

"Help! Please help!" Keenan said.

Dub scurried around looking for him while other small lights moved farther and farther away, escaping the danger.

"Keenan, where are you?"

"Down here."

Dub crawled along the ground, following the sound of Keenan's voice, moving the lantern and the light on his hat side to side. As he got closer, a sooty hand popped out of the ground. The blast had opened the ground, swallowing Keenan in the middle of his dance routine. It had blown off his hat and shirt, exposing his body to the coal mine's elements.

To break his fall, Keenan had lunged forward toward a coal cart and managed to grab one of the chains that bolted it to the track. His arms struggled to lift his body while slowly losing strength.

Dub steadied his lantern in the dirt among the fallen rocks. Lying flat on the ground, he wrapped his arms under Keenan's armpits and around his sweaty shirtless body, feeling the other man's skin torn by the rock and coal shards and projectiles from the blast.

The light from Dub's hat created an ominous vision of coal dust, sweat, and blood blended like a new coat that covered Keenan from his head down to his torso. Only the dim light made Keenan's head distinguishable from a rock on the ground.

Dub braced his elbows into the ground and pulled upward. Coal mining gave him exceptional upper body strength, enough to drag Keenan.

Between Dub's pulling and Keenan's climbing, the two men both made it to the flat surface, falling with Keenan landing on top of Dub, next to the dead canary in its cage. Both men were safe. Suddenly, two blasts echoed one after the other, the second much closer than the first.

The men looked at each other briefly, and as Dub scrambled off the ground, a large glob of mucus struck his cheek, followed by the words, "Never touch me again! I'd rather die than feel your colored skin against mine. I've killed men like you for less."

A leather boot struck the side of Dub's leg, knocking him back to the ground. Dub grabbed Keenan's ankle as the other man turned to run down the tunnel. Keenan stumbled to the ground.

The two men tussled amid the falling debris from a third blast. They could only see each other as shadows cast on the moist coal slate by the light on Dub's hat and a lantern. Keenan straddled Dub, squeezing his neck.

On the wall of the shaft, the shadow of Keenan's long torso appeared as a tall, majestic poplar tree, his arms a long rope, his hands simulating a noose around Dub's neck. Dub dug his fingernails into Keenan's hands to extract them from his throat.

Losing consciousness, he clawed at the dirt, struggling to lunge back into the fight as he had wanted to do to save Tuttle so many years earlier, when Dub was only fourteen. A lump of coal fell onto Dub's hand as the tunnel disintegrated. His fingers wrapped around the coal, and he gathered enough strength to swiftly smash the rock into Keenan's temple. Keenan fell to the ground.

"This is for my father and my son," he said, pushing Keenan with both feet, followed by a scream of desperation. "Now you suffer and die, you bastard!"

Keenan tumbled back into the crater from which he'd emerged, with nothing to grasp this time. His scream faded farther away, until it stopped. Shaken by another rumble, Dub jumped up, grabbed his lantern, and ran through the tunnels as he had twice daily each time he worked underground.

The final long dark tunnel reappeared as dust settled. No

other lights shone in view. With only the glow from his hat and the lantern, and the rail line for the coal cars as a compass, he ran quickly, avoiding boulders. When he got to the face of the mine, Mae ran toward him as she had in Morriston when he'd stood in the line to apply for the Tappers job.

Jimmy came up from behind and placed his hand on Dub's shoulder and said, "Glad you made it out. Now we just need to account for Keenan."

"I can't tell you what happened, but I heard him scream like he fell."

When he returned home the next day, Mae told Dub she was pregnant for the eighth time, and Dub told Mae about his latest promotion, to machine mining crew supervisor.

"Too bad Tim can't be more like you," Mae replied.

"I am designing my destiny, and so is Tim. I'm good now."

ACKNOWLEDGMENTS

This book would not exist without the encouragement of my father, Archibald Mosley (1925–2020). Almost every day for four months at his apartment in the assisted living center, he sat in his easy chair, closed his eyes, and listened to every chapter immediately after it was written. Sometimes I thought he was asleep, but when I stopped reading, he shared with me the visual my words painted in his mind and helped ground the characters in early twentieth-century history, the lives of his ancestors, and the climate of that time. Not once was he sleeping, however. His spirit and waning strength encouraged and guided the development of this book and its sequel. I also want to thank my mother, my first love as a newborn, Jerolene Thomas Mosley (1928–2022), who, despite her progressive dementia, read the first completed manuscript only months before she left this world. They are my angels who still guide me from my heart.

Thanks to my toughest critic, Kathleen Wilcox Pelzer, for reading the entire manuscript and giving feedback and supporting its final publication. She is the most voracious reader of novels on this planet. An additional thanks to Dr. Monica Smith and Vicki A. Miller, who provided comments on early drafts. Thanks to my cousin Harold Thomas, who gave the book a title and cheered me on. And finally, to my friend Genese Gibson, who let me know I needed to unleash the book inside me and, before a single word was written, encouraged my dream of bringing this story to print. A special acknowledgment to my daughter (journalist) and son (entrepreneur, movie producer, and writer), who showed me a return on my investment in their college educations by allowing me to send short pieces from time to time for their review and comment.

WATCH FOR BOOK 2 OF THE LOST SEEDS SERIES—YOUR MUST-READ FOR SUMMER 2024!

And as three times before over the four decades, a familiar shadow, a strut he had seen over his lifetime, sauntered up the driveway from the ruins where the shack once stood. Even sleep could not mask the dichotomy of Dub's life. Tim appeared cleaner and more confident than he had in years . . .

ABOUT THE AUTHOR

Teresa Sebastian believes spiritual words and the sounds of nature soothe the inner being and define a place of peace. Creative writing is her way to release the soul and share herself with the world. When she is not writing, Teresa is an attorney, entrepreneur, and law school professor. She seeks to make a difference in the environment and culture through her involvement with community and corporate boards.

Teresa has always been compelled to put words to the human life she sees around her. When her children were young, she made up stories about characters that traveled around the world and immersed herself in the imaginative worlds of *Sesame Street* and *Mister Rogers' Neighborhood*. She now composes children's jingles about her granddaughter and sings them to her. *Lost Seeds: The Beginning* is her first novel.

The second installment in the Lost Seeds series, about the Briscos and the next generation, is coming soon. After all . . . legacies live in stories.

For more information, visit
https://teresamosleysebastian.com.